Vanessa Gordon lives in Surrey and spent many years working in Classical music as a concert manager, musician's agent and live music supplier. She has travelled all over Greece and has visited as often as possible over the last fifteen years.

The Martin Day mystery series is set on Naxos, the largest island in the Cyclades. It is an island of contrasts. The modern port of Chora is crowned by a Venetian kastro which is surrounded by an interesting old town. On Naxos you can find uninhabited hills, the highest mountain in the Cyclades, attractive fishing villages, popular beaches and archaeological sites. There are historic towers and welcoming tavernas, collectable art and ceramics. Naxos has produced some of the finest marble in Greece since ancient times.

Now Martin Day has moved in.

BY THE SAME AUTHOR

The Meaning of Friday

The Search for Artemis

Black Acorns

Black Acorns

A Naxos mystery *with Martin Day*

Vanessa Gordon

Published by Pomeg Books 2021 www.pomeg.co.uk

Cover photograph and map © Alan Gordon

Cover image: Agia Tower, Naxos

Illustration of bronze horse by Brenda Ord

ISBN: 978-1-8384533-2-9

Pomeg Books is an imprint of
Dolman Scott Ltd
www.dolmanscott.co.uk

For Arabella and George

Warm thanks to Christine Wilding, Alan Gordon and Cristine Mackie for their invaluable proofreading, and especially to Mary Chipperfield, my friend and for many years my teacher, for hers.

My special thanks to Robert Pitt, who first introduced me to Greece and the great delights of its past, its cuisine and its wine, and who showed me the Towers of the Mani.

Most of all, thanks to Alan and Alastair for their constant love and support.

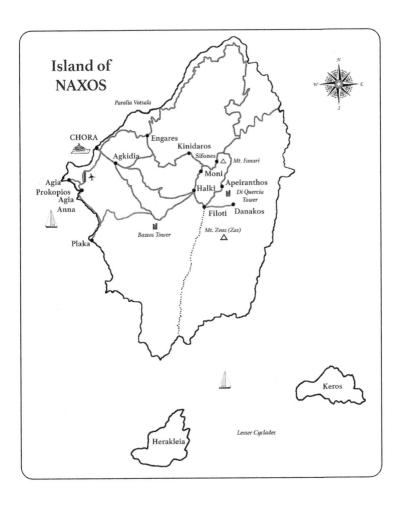

Island of
NAXOS

Paralia Votsala

CHORA
Engares
Kinidaros
Agkidia
Sifones
Mt. Fanari
Moni
Agia
Halki
Apeiranthos
Prokopios
Di Quercia
Agia
Tower
Anna
Filoti
Danakos
Bazeos Tower
Mt. Zeus (Zas)
Plaka

N
W   E
S

Keros

Herakleia

Lesser Cyclades

A NOTE ABOUT GREEK WORDS

Readers without a knowledge of Greek might like to know about one or two things that they will notice in the book.

Greek names sometimes have changed endings when the person is directly addressed. You will see Thanasis become Thanasi, Andreas become Andrea, and Aristos become Aristo.

Spellings most likely to help with pronunciation are used in this book.

The main town of Naxos is called Chora (and also Naxos). You pronounce the ch in Chora as in the Scottish 'loch'. Similarly, Halki (sometimes written as Chalki) begins with that sound.

Kyrie and *Kyria* are forms of address like monsieur and madame
Mou means my and is often used after a name as a term of affection
Agapi mou - my dear
Kali Orexi - Bon appétit
Efharisto - Thank you
Efharistoume - We thank you
Kalimera - Hello, Good morning
Kalispera - Good evening
Kalinichta - Goodnight
Kalos Irthatay! - Welcome
Ti kaneis - How are you?
Kala. Eseis? - I'm well, and you?
Stin yia sas! - Good health!
Oriste! is a common way to answer the phone.
filoxenia - traditional hospitality
estiatorio - restaurant

Paralia Votsala - bay of pebbles
mikri agora - mini market
periptero - kiosk
Agia Anna - St Anna
Agios Ioannis - St John
maquis - typical scrub vegetation
meltemi - prevailing wind in the Cyclades
elliniko kafes - Greek coffee
kitron - a large, solid citrus fruit famous on Naxos
kouneli stifado - rabbit casserole
gigantes - a dish of baked giant beans
patates fournou - roast potatoes
mezethes - small savoury bites to have with ouzo (sing. meze)
tsipouro - distilled spirit
tzatziki - yogurt, garlic and cucumber
katsikaki - baby goat
horta - green vegetables (leaves)

1

The stylish house in the foothills of the Taygetus Mountains of Greece belonged to an American in his nineties who guarded his privacy so effectively that most people did not even know his name. He had always intended to spend his final years in Greece, the country whose history and art he loved most in the world, and the area he loved the most was this mountainous part of the Peloponnese. Local builders had constructed the house to his own design in an isolated spot that he had chosen with care. The modern town of Sparta was some distance away, near enough to supply his needs, but all he could see from his house was the timeless grandeur of the landscape. The Taygetus Mountains lifted their bulk in beauty around him, and whatever the season their colours were a shifting palette of greys, blues and greens. In spring the slopes were full of wild flowers, the fields and trees alive with birds and butterflies, and in the distance he could see the sea. To the old man, a lover of Greek history, the land seemed little changed since the Ancient Spartans had lived and fought here.

The house was surrounded by an impregnable metal fence that was cleverly designed to impinge as little as possible on his view. There were two serious reasons for the perimeter security, one being the death threats that the old American had received in the past, having once stirred up the vicious envy of a group of disaffected types whose chances of making anything like his wealth were non-existent. He could never forget it, even though he had left that life behind in America.

The second reason for security was the old man's collection of treasures, once described in the US as the most unique collection of Greek antiquities in private hands. None of his friends had ever seen it. Nobody had. He had acquired his beautiful artefacts over many decades, and they were all the company he wanted now. Having always been locked away before, the collection was now displayed around the house, and the old man regularly cradled an ancient object in his hands, revelling in its loveliness and its history.

For his practical needs, he could afford to pay for live-in help. This consisted of a fifty-year-old German called Manfred. Manfred was employed as companion, cook, housekeeper and head of security. The two got on well enough, and Manfred's presence gave the old man peace of mind. They talked, they ate together, they shared life stories and lived quietly over a number of years. It was Manfred, however, who opened the gate to the thieves who stole the collection.

The American had not seriously expected ever to be robbed. He had believed his valuable collection to have been forgotten about in the busy world beyond the Taygetus, and the local people knew nothing about it. He was not hurt in the robbery, as the faithful Manfred gave him a powerful sedative. There was, however, a casualty: a local man who was taking supplies to an isolated sheep farm in the hills and who saw the robbery taking place was badly beaten by the gang and left for dead on the verge.

After the robbery, there was no sign of either Manfred or the collection. The gang had taken their time, and the German had shown them where all the treasures were to be found. The Hellas Police threw all their resources at what became known in the force as the Taygetus Raid, but although they soon guessed the identity of the thieves, they were unable to make even a single arrest. Even when a few of the stolen antiquities surfaced in Paris, New York and London, it became clear that the gang had acted cleverly so that no item led the police to their door.

Two frustrating years later the case remained unsolved, and the lack of new leads led the police to shelve the inquiry. Of his busy colleagues on the force, only Inspector Andreas Nomikos of the Athens Police, a man obsessed with international antiquity fraud relating to Greece, was never able to forget the case.

2

Archaeologist and TV presenter Martin Day, feeling every one of his thirty-nine years after a long day of filming, stood on a hillside in the Mani region of the southern Peloponnese, surrounded by the awaiting camera team. He was still wearing his sunglasses, and would only remove them when they were about to start filming again. The October sun was now low and right in his eyes. The heat from the stone wall next to him warmed his back, and an amber glow burnished the old tower houses that rose steeply behind him. Day was resigned to the delay, he was used to it by now, but he was keenly looking forward to the moment when the Director announced the end of the session. The next take would be the last, and that was what mattered: he was ready for a shower and a drink.

With a shout the Director gave the go-ahead to resume filming. Day removed his sunglasses and held them in front of him at waist level so that they could be back on his face as soon as possible. He adopted a professional smile and willed himself to make no slips, the sooner to finish the job.

"This place behind me has been called 'the most photographed village in the Mani'. Its name is Vathia, and it's one of the best surviving examples of a fortified Maniot town. Most of the houses are now abandoned, and you can walk round them absorbing a silence that resonates with the memory of more turbulent times.

"As we've already seen during this programme, many of the eight hundred or so Venetian towers here in the Mani stand alone in the hills, imposing bastions against invasion, fortified refuges in case of attack. Competition among the clans to have the highest tower was so great that the towers became taller and taller.

"Here at Vathia, we can see that domestic houses were built in a similar style, and it was done for the same reason. These 'Tower Houses', as they're called, were small strongholds, each one an impregnable refuge for members of a single family. A Tower House was built like a small castle, and sheltered people during an age of violent vendettas and bloody feuds.

"To understand the Venetian towers it's helpful to consider the landed estates of Europe and America. Not only did the estate protect the owner's wealth and family, it was a symbol of status and respectability. If the family lost ownership of the estate, or the building was allowed to degenerate, there was a very serious impact on the owners' status and future. So it was with these towers and Tower Houses.

"The Towers of the Mani, whether defensive giants like those we've been looking at in the countryside, or domestic houses like these at Vathia, are symbols of an area with a long and often violent history. The Mani is a mountainous and inaccessible part of Greece which has been inhabited since Neolithic times: a human skull discovered in a cave here is the oldest so far found in Europe. Maniots have a reputation for being tough and rebellious. In the 1820s, the mountains of the Mani became the stronghold of the Klephts, fierce bandits opposed to Ottoman rule. And the fierce spirit of the men of the

Mani is not a thing of the past, even though today the area welcomes visitors and relies to a large extent on tourism. If you drive through the region you can still see road signs peppered with bullet holes, target practice for the local young men. The Maniots claim to be directly descended from the Ancient Spartans, and their castellated towers suggest the continuation of the Spartans' combative and indomitable spirit.

"A long and fierce history, then, is embodied in the towers we have looked at in this programme. We have seen towers that are as high as twenty metres, surveying the sea from the crest of a cliff, and a complete village of Tower Houses forming a fortified community. In the next programme I'll be visiting the capital of the Mani, the modern town of Areopolis, where, true to the proud tradition of the area, the famous Petros Mavromichalis led the Greek War of Independence."

"Cut! Thanks everyone. Well done!" shouted Scott Macfarlane, the Director, sounding every bit as thankful as Day felt. "That's us done!"

Thank God, thought Day, and replaced his sunglasses. He smiled at the crew, thanked the sound engineer, and headed for the shade. His height and fair hair marked him out in the crowd and several people moved politely aside to give him access to the refreshment kiosk. He grabbed two small mineral waters and drank one as he walked away. He took the other over to the control tent where Scott was talking to two crew members, trying to bring the session to a close. He turned gratefully to Day and accepted the bottle of water.

"Thanks, Martin. Are you pleased with how it went today?"

"Yes, I think so. We did well to finish filming before we lost that good light. Vathia will look stunning lit by the low sun. Have you got everything you need?"

"It's all done. The filming we did inside Vathia this morning will provide material to cut into your longer explanations, and the pieces recorded yesterday in Areopolis were excellent. And those enormous stone towers in the countryside where we were last week are really impressive!"

"Good. When I'm in London in December give me a call, we can go through whatever you need me to re-voice. There might be a few takes in the Areopolis section which will need re-recording, I think there were some background noises in a few places, and I should probably record one bit again where I wasn't very clear. Right, I'm ready to go back to the hotel now. Can I give you a lift?"

"Fantastic, yes please. David can finish up here and join us later. I'll just have a word with him."

Scott gave instructions to David Mikos, the Anglo-Greek deputy director, and then joined Day by his hire car. The company had supplied an old Skoda, a much better fit for Day's height than the Fiat 500 he drove on Naxos, but already he hated it. The Skoda would not have been his first choice for the twisting, mountainous roads of the Mani.

They drove north-west to Gerolimena following the line of the coast, the sun still in their eyes. Scott's mind was already moving ahead.

"Are you going straight back to Naxos tomorrow, Martin?" he asked.

"Yes, assuming this worn-out wreck makes it as far as Kalamata airport. Only a hundred and ten kilometres through the Mani, what could possibly go wrong?"

They discussed work until they arrived at the hotel where the production team were staying. It was one of the most beautiful hotels Day could remember, located in a rural hamlet outside the coastal village of Gerolimena. Originally another eighteenth-century tower, it was a luxuriously converted, almost circular stone building, and was quiet just now, the main tourist season being over. Day had a ground floor room in a low-level stone annex, a room so stunning that he could have spent the whole evening in it had it not been for the even more impressive terrace bar and the prospect of good company.

He took a shower in his wet-room using the boutique toiletries provided, chose fresh clothes from the shabby chic wardrobe in his domed, stone-walled bedroom, and opened the door to allow the evening sun to flood through the doorway. He sat on the end of the vast double bed that awaited him later and sent a text to Helen saying he would be back on Naxos the next day, but would take a taxi home from the port. That done, he set out to claim a table on the terrace and await Scott.

He chose a small marble table just far enough from the tower to give him a good view of it. Uplit by orange floodlights that gilded the stone facade, the main building was almost entirely windowless; only a few slits relieved the austerity of the curved wall. An adjacent stone arch invited visitors into an interior courtyard within which a modern wooden staircase led to the hotel reception on the first floor. The stone storeys of Maniot towers were originally connected by wooden staircases, and Day was pleased to see that this style had been followed in the renovation of the building. He sat back in his chair and enjoyed the peacefulness of the terrace. A white cat strode with erect tail towards him, went straight past with a dismissive air, threw itself down on a warm flagstone and stretched out, tucking its tail round its back legs. Even when Scott emerged from his room at the far end of the hotel and joined Day at the table, the cat chose not to stir.

Like a miracle, a soft-footed young Greek approached to take their drinks order. It was rare for Day to choose anything other than his favourite, gin and tonic, and this evening was no exception; Scott ordered the same. Once they had their drinks, Day declared himself in Paradise.

"So, what have you got lined up next, Scotty?" he asked, when he had savoured his drink for a moment.

"My next job? I'm taking a team to Portugal in a fortnight to film a programme on Coimbra Pottery for the Secrets of Art people. You should look into working with them yourself, Martin. They'd welcome you with open arms."

"Coincidentally, I think that's going to happen this winter, in London."

"Really? What's the subject? Have you finished the Nikos Elias book?"

"Yes, the Elias biography is with my agent now and should be published next year some time. I had the chance to make some programmes on the art of Greek marble sculpture, but we haven't managed to secure the rights to use the material yet. Meanwhile something else came up. It's a commission to do a book for the British Museum on part of their Greek ceramics collection, and there's been some talk about doing a programme on the same material with Secrets of Art. I'll be working with Alex Harding-Jones."

"Alex from the British Museum?"

"That's right. You know him, surely?"

"I met him a few years ago. Ours is a small world. Give him my best when you see him. So, what else has been happening in your life, Martin? My god, this is the first time we've been able to sit down and catch up since we got here ten days ago."

Scott settled back in his chair and stretched out his legs, prepared to enjoy an entertaining narrative if one was available. His friend was usually good for a story or two.

"Oh, it's been an exciting year," said Day, smiling into his glass, taking a sip of the Elixir of the Gods and recalling the unusually dramatic events that had distracted him since he bought his house on Naxos. "Where shall I start?"

The narrative was indeed entertaining, exactly as Scott had hoped. When they finally went to find some dinner, Scott wondered aloud whether that would be the last of Day's adventures.

3

The ferry *Blue Star Delos* brought Day home to Naxos at six o'clock the following evening. The ship turned neatly just outside the port and reversed into the mooring with only a modicum of black smoke and the required three short blasts on the horn. It lowered its vast metal gangway with a screech and final resounding crash, before emptying its load of cars, trucks and lorries onto the port. Foot passengers dragging luggage shared the gangway with vans and motorbikes. Chaos, in its most good-natured form, once again brought people to the island of Naxos.

Never completely happy until back on dry land, Day's spirits were improving and he was considering a quick stop at his favourite bar, Diogenes, before finding a taxi, when he saw a fair-haired woman standing next to a dirty white Fiat 500. She was waving at him. Helen had met the ferry. A rush of pleasure filled him. Much as he loved living alone and was quite happy to occupy and amuse himself, he had been really enjoying the last few months during which Helen, his novelist friend from England, had been staying with him.

"This is very good of you," he said, forcing his case into the boot of his car and turning to give her a short hug. "I haven't seen an available taxi anywhere. Let's escape this madness and go home."

Day folded himself into the passenger seat and began to relax. As they drove the twenty kilometres to the house, he told her about his experiences in the Mani. The road climbed away from the shore, passing through the villages that lay between the port and the hilly centre of the island. The village of Filoti, where Day had found his ideal house and bought it earlier in the year, lay not far from the island's highest peak, Mount Zas. Day loved its rural tranquility. Anyone who knew him only as a TV presenter, when he was at his most extrovert, would have been surprised to hear that he was something of a loner. Day craved peace and quiet; he enjoyed long periods of solitary research and writing, companionable silences and the gentle conversation of good friends. On the death of his father, Day had used his inheritance to buy the Filoti house, a restored island home which he described as being 'in the middle of nowhere on an island in the Aegean'. He saw it as a place of escape from the studio apartment he owned in busy Athens. He no longer had a home in the UK. Helen had been staying with him since the early summer, the two of them companionable but independent, meeting from time to time over coffee, drinks and meals.

The house smelt good to Day when he walked in: the usual aromas of old polished wood, clean country air, and a faint hint of wild herbs. He opened the shutters and the early October warmth filled the front room. He left his case in the middle of the floor and went through to the back room, lined with his bookcases, and opened the windows and shutters of the balcony. The view across the valley to the further hills was even better than he remembered. October had arrived, bringing the muted ochres of bleached grass, orange-gold lichen and yellow-green, desiccated scrub.

He heard the unmistakable sound of a kettle and smiled. Helen was making tea. Fair enough, he thought. A cup of tea first, and then a gin.

He took his suitcase to his room and took the fastest shower possible before putting on fresh clothes and returning to the balcony. Helen was already sitting with a cup of tea, her brown arms and sun-bleached hair a sign of having spent many months on the island, which had transformed her skin from Hampstead white to Aegean bronze. He settled into the chair next to hers.

"That's better," he said, drinking his tea. "It's wonderful to be back. How have you been?"

"Fine. I sent off the novel to my agent on Wednesday, so it's off my hands at last."

"That's great! We must celebrate tonight with a meal at the taverna. Are you pleased with how it turned out?"

"Yes, I suppose so." She quickly corrected her tone. "I'm quite pleased with it. I didn't know what to do with myself after it went off with the courier. Then oddly, just at the right moment, a man called *Kyrie* Tsirmpas rang me, the chairman of the Naxos Literary Festival. He offered me a job."

"I thought the Literary Festival was already in progress?"

"Yes it is, but somebody had to pull out, Nikos Kounaras, the poet from Thasos, who was going to be their Writer in Residence. His wife went into labour early, apparently! Our friend Aristos at the Museum gave them my name and they asked me to step in and help."

"Aristos has his fingers in every pie on the island. What does your job involve?"

"They want me to be present for most of the sessions, sometimes acting as a group coordinator, and doing one or two interviews with visiting speakers. I'm also giving the last lecture of the Festival. Thankfully there isn't an event every day."

"Congratulations, Helen, that's excellent. Writer in Residence! They couldn't have found anyone better for the job. Don't you think it will be a lot of fun?"

"I hope so. It's perfectly timed for me, I need something to do."

"Have you met a woman called Athina yet? She's the festival manager and I've been speaking to her quite a bit while I was away because they needed extra accommodation, so she's using rooms at the Elias House."

"I've spoken to her once."

"She sounds quite a character, doesn't she? I must go and meet her tomorrow, and find out more about the guests."

The sprawling Elias House was a large place by the sea formerly owned by the late Nikos Elias, the Greek archaeologist whose biography Day had recently completed. Having not known what use to make of the old place when it became his property, he had converted it into simple but spacious visitor accommodation. The Literary Festival was providing his very first guests.

"How many rooms have been booked?"

"Two doubles and a single, I think. Our friends Vasilios and Maroula from the taverna have prepared the rooms, and Athina has sorted out the bookings. Right, how about I make us a gin and tonic?"

He went to the galley kitchen and returned with his signature drink. A strong smell of lemon came with him, rising from the icy glasses that brimmed with bubbles.

"Delicious! I haven't had a G&T since you left for the Mani."

"Are you OK?" he teased, but he had noted an uncharacteristic despondency in her voice, which even he could not miss.

"I'm fine." Helen hesitated before continuing reluctantly. "Andreas has been pestering me. He emails most days, and wants me to go and see him in Athens. I was tempted to go, it would have been nice to spend a few days in Athens, but I didn't want Andreas to think that our relationship is going to start up again." She smiled. "Don't worry, Martin, I'm just a bit low. And here I am on an idyllic Cycladic island with everything I could possibly want."

Day smiled with her, evaluating the reference to Andreas. Andreas Nomikos, the police inspector from Athens, was proving not only a most unusual detective but a rather determined suitor. He and Helen had begun to see each other a few months before, but at some point Day had realised that Helen had put the brakes on the relationship. He doubted Andreas would give up easily. He waited for her to say more.

"I suppose when I think of Andreas I remember Zissis. You'd think my marriage was a thing of the past, wouldn't you? Zissis died six years ago, and I heard nothing from him for twelve years before that, but Andreas stirs up the memories again because I swore never to get into another relationship. Sorry, you've heard this so many times!"

"You're welcome to tell me whenever you want."

Day was only too aware of his deficiencies as a listener, not helped by a recurring urge to hit Helen's ex-husband despite never actually having met him. As the man was now dead he should help Helen to forget him, of course, but unfortunately the past was not so easily left behind. Helen had married the Greek financier in her early twenties, but soon he had realised that a wife was an encumbrance to the life he most enjoyed. He had bought her a house in Hampstead and provided enough money for her to live comfortably, because wealth was something Zissis did not lack. Despite not having the divorce which his religion forbade him, he had then led a self-indulgent life with his immense fortune and many women until his relatively early death. When Day had met Helen she was alone in London with only sorrow and anger for company.

Helen replaced her glass on the wooden table firmly.

"I'd like to ask you something, Martin. Would you mind if I stayed on here a bit longer than planned? I don't want to go back to Hampstead yet. Perhaps I could travel to London with you when you go in a couple of months. You're very welcome to stay at my place while you work at the British Museum over the winter."

Day agreed immediately; it was, in fact, a proposal that suited him really well. Anyway, he was glad there was something he could do for her. Helen was usually the one who lifted his mood, not the other way round. Hers was the level-headed voice of common sense which he would consult before almost any difficult decision. She was his ideal best friend, a woman who could be relied on not to want any romantic involvement with him that would distract him from his work.

"How often do you think about Zissis these days?" he ventured, not sure if this was a good path to take.

Helen glanced at him in surprise. "Well, not very often, but the past never really goes away, does it? You of all people have to agree to that, Martin, as an archaeologist!"

"I had an idea on the plane this morning," he said, a convenient opener although not strictly true. "I thought I might invite Alex over for a couple of days? It would be good for us to make a start on our British Museum book, and it would be fun. What do you think?"

"Good idea. Why don't you ask him?" she said, her smile back in place, picking up her glass.

"Right, I'll call him tomorrow. Come on, let's go for dinner. Thanasis must have been missing us."

They walked into Filoti in the evening light past battered old cars faded from the sun and covered in dust. Elderly neighbours sat in front of their houses, talking to each other across the street and playing absentmindedly with their komboloi beads. Several people waved to Day and called out *Kalispera!* He smiled as he returned the greeting, feeling that he was slowly being accepted as a member of the village community.

Taverna O Thanasis, which had long been Day's favourite local restaurant, was the first building on the right on the road into the village. As usual, they were greeted warmly by the owner himself. Thanasis was a large man, understandably so given the outstanding culinary skills of his wife, and he had a wide smile to match. He kissed Helen on both cheeks, addressing her as usual as 'La Belle Helene'. He loved it when she protested, and laughed contentedly as he showed them to their usual table. Just the sight of the blue tablecloths, the traditional wooden chairs with woven seats, and the sepia photographs on the walls filled Day with joy at being back on Naxos. Vangelis, son of Thanasis, came over to place menus in front of them.

"Good evening, Vangeli," Day said, shaking the younger man's hand and leaving the menus unopened. "What's on the special menu tonight?"

Although the regular dishes were always good, the best thing to do was to ask what the cook recommended. Thanasis's wife, Koula, created dishes each day inspired by ingredients from local farmers and fishermen. It was a wise customer who chose these little masterpieces.

"My mother recommends the *katsikaki* today, or she has some fresh bream which you can have grilled or fried. She has made fried zucchini slices and eggplant balls using her mother's recipes - they're wonderful! - and we have freshly-picked *horta* today. Horta are green leaves grown locally ...."

Day grinned and nodded. Horta was a favourite, its straggly dark green leaves full of freshness and flavour.

Vangelis smiled widely and said that he would let them consider while he brought their wine. He did not even ask what wine they wanted, being well aware of Day's usual choice. He returned with a large jug of the local red wine 'from the barrel', fresh and light, and particularly welcome because it was unlikely to give you a bad head the next day.

"What shall we eat? Your choice," said Day, when they were alone. He took her glass and added some wine, gave her some cutlery from the bread basket, and filled his own glass.

"Mmm. Fish and vegetables for me, I think. Bream, some *horta*, and the little aubergine balls."

"Ok, suits me, and maybe a portion of chips?"

Day loved chips and had the perfect excuse to enjoy them on the island because the people of Naxos were very proud of their potatoes. No visitor could avoid hearing of the unique flavour and texture of Naxian potatoes, and Day hardly missed an opportunity to put this assertion to the test. He had never been disappointed.

They shared the dishes between them and ate with relish without touching on any serious subjects of conversation. Helen expertly opened the grilled fish and separated the soft white flesh from the bones, before helping herself to a few of the small, deep-fried balls of aubergine and sliding the chips closer to Day. When the last chip had gone, and no flesh remained on the bream, Day used the last slice of bread to clean the little bowl of *tzatziki* that had come with the fried vegetables, and waved to Vangelis to bring another small jug of wine.

"Now," he said to Helen, "Can I attend any events at this Literary Festival? I'd like to see you in action! It's all being held at the Bazeos Tower, isn't it, not very far from here?"

"Of course, if you like, Martin. I'll make sure you can come to all the interesting bits."

"Fantastic! I'm also hoping to meet some of the writers. One of them's quite well known, I think. Have you heard of Ricky Somerset?"

"Of course! He was nominated for the Winterson Prize for Fiction last year. I think he lives in Brighton. I've heard him called the twenty-first century's answer to Graham Green."

"Oh, right! Athina told me that he and his partner have booked a room in the Elias House. I tell you what's really odd. I recognised the name of his partner, Ben Lear. We knew each other a long time ago."

They were interrupted by Vangelis with their jug of wine.

"Did you know him well?" Helen asked.

"Pretty well. We saw a lot of each other in our teens because my father fell in love with Ben's mother. Ben was the only good thing in the whole situation, actually. As you know, I was an only child and my mother died when I was ten. After a few years my father met Julia and she and her son spent a lot of time at our house. Ben was about four years younger than me but he was fun. After I left for university I never saw Ben again because I hardly went home. My father and Julia were close till he died, but they never married. I don't know what Ben did after I left. I don't even know if Julia is still alive. The thing is, it was my fault that my father and Julia didn't marry. I put such pressure on my father not to betray my mother's memory, as I saw it. It's a long story and tonight isn't the right time."

Helen had heard him out in silence and when she spoke he half expected a rebuke.

"Well, you must talk to Ben properly while he's here, Martin," she said firmly, sounding back to her old form. "You've just described something important and unresolved in your life. This is an opportunity to try and sort it out."

4

Day was looking forward to speaking to his old friend Alex. Alex was an expert on Greek ceramics on the staff of the British Museum, and they had worked together quite often at one time, in the days before Day moved to Greece. When Day's new agent, Maurice Atkinson, had started to find Day good work in Greece and persuaded him to expand his activities as a broadcast presenter, all that had changed.

As Greek time was two hours ahead of the UK, Day had the pleasure of a slow start to his morning. At eleven thirty he took his phone to his room and smiled as he brought up Alex's mobile number. Their collaboration would be fun, and if Alex agreed to drop everything now and come to Naxos, even better.

"Alex? This is Martin. Is this a good time? Nine-thirty there, is it? I trust I've caught you on a coffee break?"

"What exactly is a coffee break? Something Greek? Good to hear from you, Martin. Hard to believe you're up this early."

"It's nearly noon over here, remember? You know I don't do early. So, what's the British weather like at the moment? Dismal and grey? Why don't you come out to Naxos for a few days? You can stay at my place. I think we should start planning the book. Come this week if you can. Helen and I will show you a good time on sunny Naxos."

Alex chuckled down the line.

"You freelancers think it's so easy to drop everything! OK, it's very tempting, and sensible to start work on the book. I'll see what I can do. I'll have to try and move a few appointments…"

"Great, come as soon as you like."

"I'm getting excited already. What's happening in your world, then?"

"I've just finished a bit of filming in the Mani, and the Nikos Elias book is finally off my hands. The Greek marble series that I told you about has been shelved, but it might come to something next year. I'm already focussing on our book for the Museum. Helen's fine, her novel has gone to the publisher. What else? Do you remember the fiasco the last time you were here, and the house owned by Nikos Elias? I now legally own that house, and I've turned it into accommodation. I've got some writers staying in it who are here for the Literary Festival. Oh, and talking of the festival, Helen is the Writer in Residence."

"You have been busy! I'm very pleased for Helen too. I'll buy a copy of the new book when it's published."

They chatted for a while. Day heard something in his friend's tone that told him Alex would soon come to Naxos. How could the British Museum possibly object to their Bronze Age specialist making a work-related trip to Greece? They might even pay for his flights.

"I'll be in touch, Martin," finished Alex eventually. "Let me know if you want me to bring anything out for you from home. Bye."

Home. The word had an odd ring to it.

Day had missed a call from a local friend, Nick Kiloziglou, and listened to his voicemail. It was an invitation for that afternoon to look at a piece of restoration work in the town's medieval area, the Kastro. Nick was an Australian Greek and the owner of a company which restored heritage buildings. He had been working on one of the most famous old buildings in the Kastro, the Della Rocca-Barozzi Tower, which housed a museum and in which a music festival took place every summer. Although well restored many years ago, money had been found for Nick's company to do some further work on the levels below the museum. Day had once mentioned that he would be interested to see the result, and today was his chance.

He smiled when he reached the end of the message. Nick suggested that he and Helen should meet him at the tower at two o'clock, and that after seeing the work they could all meet Deppi for coffee in Chora. Day quickly accepted.

Despina, known as Deppi, was Nick's wife and inconveniently Day was besotted with her. It was a good thing that Helen would be there, he thought. Helen had more than an inkling of his feelings for Deppi. Although Day had every intention of behaving perfectly, knowing that Helen's keen eye was upon him would make sure that he didn't even waver.

Helen greeted the invitation with undisguised delight. It was just the diversion she needed.

Nick was standing by the door of the Della Rocca-Barozzi Tower when Helen and Day walked through the Great Gate. An impressive, privately owned mansion within the Kastro of Naxos, the tower had been built by the Venetians who once ruled the island, and had no fewer than four underground levels. Nick led them towards the entrance to these cellars to show them the work that his restorers had just completed.

Day knew the upper floor well: it housed the Venetian Museum of Naxos and contained displays of folkloric furniture, clothes and artefacts from the centuries during which the family and their ancestors had lived in the building. Helen might enjoy it, he admitted, but he himself was more interested in the building itself and was pleased to descend to the lower levels. They entered a space built with marble and stone which dated from the thirteenth century, an intimate and atmospheric venue for art exhibitions and concerts in the summer months. They followed Nick onwards to another vaulted area where his contractors had been working.

"I met the owner this morning to show him the work, and he was pleased, I think. These arches and those niches needed some repair, and over there we completely renovated the decoration on the ceiling."

"Great job, Nick," said Day. "It's very good, looks like original work."

Day loved the Venetian towers of Naxos and had read quite a lot of the history surrounding them. The powerful Venetian navy had protected the island from pirates and built these towers as lookouts, guard posts and command centres. A few of them had been castles for important families. The Della Rocca-Barozzi tower also fulfilled two functions, now being both a museum and a family home. As Nick told them about the restoration work in detail, Day allowed the engineering terminology to wash over him while murmuring his appreciation and allowing the spirit of the distant past to seep into him from the old stone walls.

"It's a music venue too, of course. They have a piano here that was once played by Leonard Bernstein, did you know that?" Nick's Australian accent was suddenly rather noticeable and slightly incongruous in the setting, dragging Day back from the thirteenth century. "They have every kind of music here from classical trios and jazz piano to the toumbaki and tsampouna."

"What on earth are they?" laughed Helen before she could stop herself.

"The toumbaki is a drum and the tsampouna is a wind instrument like a bagpipe made from goatskin. I don't know much about them myself, Helen. Perhaps we should visit the Museum of Greek Musical Instruments in Athens."

Helen gave him a look which suggested this was not her immediate priority, and the big Greek-Australian laid a hand on her shoulder.

"Seen enough, guys? Let's grab a coffee with Deppi." He waved goodbye to the tower's owner, whom he happened to glimpse as they climbed the stairs to street level. "It's a really special place, this tower. It's been a real privilege to work here. Haven't you been making a programme about the Venetian towers in the Mani, Martin?"

As Day told the story of his work in the Mani they re-emerged into the sunshine of the outside world and walked towards the café where Deppi would be waiting for them.

Deppi was sitting at a table outside the Café Kitron looking down at her phone, oblivious of their approach. It gave Day time to pull himself together, control the delight that was surging through him, and wave Helen politely in front of him into the café.

Deppi was a small woman with long, dark hair that she usually twisted up and pinned loosely to the back of her head. Originally from the nearby island of Syros, she had met Nick while visiting her relatives in Australia, and Nick had lost little time in following her back to Greece. Day could understand why.

She got up with a smile when she saw them and they all exchanged kisses on both cheeks, pulled out chairs and arranged themselves round the table. Day ordered his usual frappé and idly stirred it for a long time while listening abstractedly to the conversation. Helen told them about having finished her novel, her manner conveying nothing but contentment, carefully concealing the uncharacteristic mood swings of which Day was aware. Then she asked the Greek couple when they planned to move into their new house in Plaka village. Once an old shell of a building, Nick was making it into their family home. While the work was ongoing, they were living on a beautiful yacht in the harbour which they had bought some time ago as an investment to give tourist tours round the local islets during the high season.

"Moving day can't come soon enough," answered Deppi, rolling her eyes. "The wind has been making life on the *Zephyro* very uncomfortable recently, and Nestoras hasn't slept well at all, which means we've all had disturbed nights. I'm so looking forward to living on dry land again. At least the house is really taking shape at last. You must both come over as soon as we move in."

She looked from Helen to Day to emphasise her invitation, and he could think of nothing to say. He held her eyes longer than necessary, and it was he who eventually looked away. Deppi smiled and turned back to Helen to answer a question about her ten year old son, Nestoras. Day's attention was drawn back to her. The tenderness between Deppi and her son had been what had first attracted him.

"Have you got more work lined up, Martin?" Nick asked, bringing Day back to earth.

"Yes, I'll be compiling a book on the more unusual Greek ceramics in the British Museum. I'm doing the work with my old friend Alex Harding-Jones, and it's likely that we'll also make a short film to accompany the book as a DVD. How about you? What's next after the work in the Kastro?"

"Ah! A real plum of a job, Martin, the kind that doesn't come along very often. It's the complete restoration of one of the ruined towers in the centre of the island. What's left of the exterior seems sound enough, but the interior walls and floors have crumbled away. The owners want it restored for family accommodation, high spec and respecting the tradition of the building. It's an amazing opportunity to work on such a project."

"That's great, Nick. What tower is it?"

Day's interest in Naxos's old towers extended to the ruined ones, and he had begun to research Naxos's dilapidated but still astonishing structures. There were surprisingly many of them. Most dated from the seventeenth century, when the new but mostly absent Ottoman owners of Naxos left in charge the efficient Venetians who had already ruled the place for over three centuries. Venetian construction consequently flourished. He recognised the name when Nick told him.

"It's called the Di Quercia Tower. Not many people have even heard of it. It's off the road and easy to miss unless you know it's there, in the hills between Filoti and Apeiranthos. The owners are the Di Quercia family of Venice. They originally came from Naxos but made their money in Italy. My client is Signora Di Quercia, who is now the head of the family, a very well-educated woman; she's done her homework on the place and knows what she wants."

"It sounds a huge project," said Helen, "and an expensive one."

"Too right," grinned Nick. "But it will pay off for her in the end. It's going to be the most amazing place."

5

Day was not known for being a morning person, and today was no exception. He reached out of bed for his phone to check the time. He had slept in. His room was fragrant with the fresh island air because he had left the window open rather than use the air conditioning. The Cyclades were cooler than the mainland, and since October had now brought autumn to Naxos, the oppressive heat of high summer had eased.

He swung his legs out of bed and went for his shower, turning on the iron which stood ready on the ironing board. Only two clean shirts left, he really must make an effort with his laundry. Tomorrow, maybe.

He turned his face into the trickle of warm water from the shower and began to feel more awake. With his eyes shut he smiled at the memory of Deppi Kiloziglou, taking an almost innocent pleasure in recalling her long look the previous afternoon. Then, banishing the image and turning off the shower in the same movement, he dried himself and went to iron a shirt. He had arranged to meet the manager of the Naxos Literary Festival, Athina, for the first time, at the Elias House which now accommodated guests from the Festival. He chose his shirt with care.

As he dressed he reflected yet again with some disbelief on how he had come to be the owner of three homes in Greece. Over fifteen years ago he had moved to his tiny apartment in Athens. It had been left to him by elderly friends of his father, who had bought it in the days when property was cheap in what was now one of the best areas of the city. Day had lived there happily for many years, never thinking beyond the present. His career as a freelance archaeologist earned him just enough to maintain his modest lifestyle. Even when he found his London agent and work began to be more lucrative, the studio apartment still suited him.

Then last year his father had passed away. Day had struggled to know what best to do with the house in Tunbridge Wells where he had grown up. Then he had realised for the first time that his future lay not in England but in Greece, and so he had sold his father's house and bought the place on Naxos, in Filoti. This left him without a base in England, which brought its own problems, but he could ignore them for a while.

Two places in Greece had been enough for Day and he had not sought to own the Elias House: it had been left in his charge. All that had been asked of him in return was the completion of the biography of Nikos Elias which he had been researching at the time. The conversion of the big house, which had once been a museum of Elias's work, into accommodation for scholars, artists and writers, seemed fitting.

He realised that his mood had darkened again and he had lost the benefits of his shower.

"Morning!" called Helen from the balcony as Day emerged from his room, his shirt still warm from the iron. "There's coffee in the kitchen."

He poured himself a coffee and took it out to sit with her. The morning was fresh and gentle. The view from the balcony lacked the clarity of July and August, lit now by a softer October sun as Greece cruised towards winter. Helen pointed across the valley at a shepherd who was walking with his sheepdog towards the higher slopes to attend to his sheep. The figures were so distant as to be virtually invisible to Day.

"You're very observant," Day reflected. "Do you think it's because you're a writer?"

"I suppose we see what interests us," she murmured, and drank some more coffee. "You're quite observant yourself when it comes to unravelling these puzzles that you insist on trying to solve."

"I'm done with all that," Day said. "I don't expect to get involved with anything like it again."

Helen said nothing.

"I'm going over to the Elias House to meet Athina at eleven. Do you want to come? We could have lunch at Taverna Ta Votsala afterwards and stay for a chat with Vasilios and Maroula."

"I can't today, sorry. I agreed to help Deppi clean up the new house. It needs a good going over before they can move in and I said I'd give her a hand. She's picking me up at noon."

"Oh," said Day. He didn't know why he felt so deflated suddenly. He drank the rest of his coffee in one go and got up to make another pot. "No problem," he said.

Cheered by strong coffee, Day sang snatches of Gilbert and Sullivan as he drove westward across the island, heading for the house where he had spent many long days working on his biography of Nikos Elias.

Paralia Votsala, a wide bay largely undiscovered by visitors, could only be accessed via a steeply-descending track off the main Engares to Apollonas coast road. Invisible from the main road, the track ended abruptly at the shingle beach and the azure Aegean sea. A right turn would take you to the taverna owned by Day's friend, Vasilios Papathoma; the road to the left led to the house that had once belonged to Nikos Elias, its white-painted walls wedged between the cliff and the sea.

Day drove to up the house and parked his car between a Fiat that matched his own but for a hire company logo, and a red Suzuki Jimny that showed signs of the wear and tear suffered by all the cars on the island. He wondered which one belonged to Athina.

The straggly bougainvillea that he rather liked was still fighting pluckily for life in the rusty barrel by the front door. The old sign announcing the Nikos Elias Museum was gone, probably thanks to Vasilios; he would have to find someone to make a new sign for his guest house.

The door opened before he reached it and an attractive young woman came towards him. She wore a large smile which revealed perfect teeth, and a short red dress. Her long hair, parted in the middle and warmed by blonde highlights, was what Day particularly noticed as he prepared to respond to her greeting.

"Martin? You *must* be Martin! I'm Athina Kalogiannis. Good to meet you at last."

Day shook her hand and they leaned in to each other to exchange the traditional two-cheek kiss.

"I'm sorry we couldn't meet sooner," he said. "I had work on the mainland."

"Yes, you told me on the phone. Making a film! It must have been very hot work."

She laughed as she said it, with a brief glance at the sunburn on his forehead. With a reassuring hand on his left arm she guided him into the house in front of her, talking all the time. Her English was really excellent, so good that Day wondered whether she was bilingual.

"I've made a list of your guests with their contact details, which rooms they've booked, for how long, and the payment information of course. I'll transfer the deposits when you give me your bank details, and I'll arrange to collect the balance from their cards before their departure. Let's sit down in the study and I'll go through it with you."

She led him through the cool house to the small room at the back which Day had used as his office when he was doing his research. Athina had taken over the room and there was now no sign that Day had ever been there. He accepted the guest chair she offered him, and she herself took the seat behind his desk.

"Let me tell you about your guests. I'm afraid there's a distinct lack of gorgeous single ladies, Martin. Better luck next time! So, in the blue room at the back of the house there is Melanie Savage. Mrs Savage writes literary fiction and is going to give a short talk at the Festival about her latest novel, *An Ode to Tedona*. I'm afraid I had to be told that the title is a palindrome, is that the right word? To be honest, Martin, I didn't know what a palindrome was till Mrs Savage explained. Apparently, you can read the title equally well either forwards or backwards! Why would you want to do that? I think her books are probably too clever for me! Nice woman, though.

"In the room at the front you have a couple from Italy. The husband is the writer, and his wife has come for the beach. David Worthington is the husband's name, he's actually English but they live in Puglia. His wife is Italian, Elissa. David is gorgeous! He writes psychological thrillers, I'm sure they're terrifying, but he's a lamb.

"Then there's our most famous author, Ricky Somerset. I mentioned him on the phone, didn't I? He's about the same age as you. Apparently he also teaches English as a foreign language, and his partner, husband actually I think, is a jazz pianist. I've put them in the biggest room overlooking the sea."

"Thank you so much, Athina, I'm in your debt. Have you photocopied the passports and done all the required things for the tourist authorities, or do I need to do that?"

"All done. I've given you all the details in this document, so you can do it next time without too much trouble. You've got a good house here, Martin, it will bring in a good income for you. And thanks very much for letting me use it for Festival guests; we had an amazing response and ended up with more delegates than we had accommodation."

"It's my pleasure. Are the events going well so far?"

"Really well. We've had our first guest speaker, and the rest of the time the groups have met to discuss ideas, sometimes topic-led, sometimes not. It's quite a challenge, given we have over sixty delegates, but the Bazeos Tower is the most amazing venue."

"And you're in overall charge?"

Athina laughed, a pretty, proud laugh that Day found attractive.

"I'm just in charge of the administration, Martin. They call me the General Manager. The Festival Committee has arranged all the events, the speakers and the final awards. It's a really well-organised conference and I'm sure it will become a regular highlight on Naxos."

"Where did you work before this job?"

"I'm actually employed by the Naxos Tourist Office to lead tours of the island's historic sites, but when this came up I persuaded them to give it to me."

"So you deal with visitors all the time. That explains your good English," said Day. "You must know a lot about Naxos history, then?"

"Quite a bit. I particularly like the strange stories and historic scandals! Maybe I could write a book too."

They laughed, and Day realised he was staring. Athina Kalogiannis would be an excellent tourist guide: the visitors would inevitably hang on her every word.

"You must share some scandal with me over a drink one day," he said. "I want to thank you for all your work setting this up while I was away. But now, it would be great to see if any of the guests are around? I'd like to meet them."

"It's a free day at the Festival, an opportunity for private writing or exploring the island," Athina said, "so you might be lucky. Let's go and see."

She locked the study behind her, handed the document and the keys to Day, and led the way to the room that had once been the main room of the Elias Museum and was now a sitting room for the guests. Nobody was there.

"That's a shame," said Athina. "Nearly everyone seems to be out. Let's try the beach."

They went outside and looked across the beach to where two men were sitting on the warm sand and talking. One of them looked up and waved. He stood and came towards them, followed by his companion.

They were exactly the people Day had been hoping to find, though he was not sure he was prepared.

"Martin!" said the younger man without introduction. He was short and plump, with curly hair, glasses and an innocent smile.

This was unmistakably Ben Lear, Julia's son. Had things turned out differently between Julia and his father, they could have been stepbrothers. Ben looked just as Day remembered him from when Day was eighteen and Ben fourteen. Over twenty years had passed. The smile was the same, remarkably good teeth. Gentle, dark eyes and a soft voice. Day held out his hand, and Ben Lear shook it. His fingers were long, which Day had never noticed before. Jazz pianist, Athina had told him. It made sense.

"Hello, Ben," he said. He couldn't think what else to say; his mind rejected everything that occurred to him, especially 'Long time no see'.

"Martin, this is my husband Ricky. Ricky, this is Martin, I told you we knew each other when we were kids."

Day was still thinking of Ben even as he shook hands with the famous Ricky Somerset. He was trying to remember if he had ever even wondered whether Ben was gay, and was certain that he hadn't. Ben had just been his friend. Day had not even realised that Ben was musical, and now here he was earning a living playing the piano.

Ricky Somerset, on the other hand, cheerfully wore his sexuality on his sleeve. Confidence radiated from him. He was slender where Ben was chubby, but otherwise they looked similar. Ricky's most striking features were his eyes, which seemed watchful and critical, but at the same time invited you to trust him. On the whole, Day felt, they were a couple who looked well together. He remembered what Helen had told him, and congratulated the writer on his recent award nomination. It was met with a modesty which surprised him.

"This is a fabulous house, Martin," continued Ricky. His voice was expressive, melodious even. With a sweep of the arm Ricky took in the wide bay, the cliffs behind and the old white house that had once been a line of fisherman's cottages, probably with a long history of smuggling. "The whole place is just perfect. The bay's called Paralia Votsala, isn't it? What does that mean in English?"

"*Paralia* is beach, *votsala* are little stones. Pebble Beach, if you like. Not quite on the same scale as its Californian namesake! Have you done any exploring yet? Tried the taverna over there?"

"We've definitely discovered the taverna," confirmed Ben. "We love it over there. The owner is very friendly too, and he's been telling us the history of this house."

"Ah. Athina is the person to talk to about local history," said Day, who was keen to avoid a conversation about the recent past of the Elias House. "Is this your first visit to Naxos?"

There was a moment of hesitation as Ben glanced at Ricky as if checking something he hadn't asked before.

"First time for both of us," said Ricky with a laugh.

"Are you enjoying the Festival, Ricky?"

"I'm really loving it. It's all very well organised, but of course the best part is getting to know the other writers. I've not been to anything like this before, where the event is spread over such a long period. It's great, it gives you time to settle in, get to know people and really benefit from the group."

Athina gave Ricky her warmest smile before turning to Ben.

"How about you, Ben?" she said. "I can tell you where you can hear some good local music, if you like?"

"That would be wonderful, thanks," said Ben. "So far I've been dropping Ricky at the Bazeos Tower and driving round the island exploring. It's a larger island that I thought, and the villages have such character."

"Have you walked round the Kastro yet?" asked Day. "If not, you must, there's a lot to see. I heard there's a piano there that was once played by Bernstein. Maybe they'd let you play it. Athina will give you the details."

Day suddenly felt it was time for him to leave.

"Well, I need to get back. I expect I'll see you at the Festival, Ricky. And maybe we could have a catch-up sometime, Ben, if you fancy? I'll send you a text, if I may?"

Ben's face flushed and he nodded. "I'd like that, Martin."

6

"Good morning, Mr Day. Are you here to see the Curator?"

"Yes, if he's not busy."

"I'll just check with him."

The receptionist at the Naxos Archaeological Museum picked up the desk phone and pressed a button. After a few words he replaced the handset and told Day to go up to the Curator's office.

Day took the wide stone steps two at a time with the enthusiasm of a younger man. It was part of his approach to turning forty that he made himself run up escalators and take steps at speed. The only thing he always did at a slow pace, apart from get up in the morning, was drive. Given the twisting mountain roads on the island, that was definitely a good thing.

His friend Aristos Iraklidis, the museum curator, occupied an office on the top floor. The Naxos Museum was housed in another Venetian building in the Kastro, one which had originally been a Jesuit School.

It contained finds from many eras of the island's history, especially from the Early Cycladic and Mycenaean periods, and a notable Roman floor mosaic. Day had spent many happy hours studying the contents of this place. There were some extraordinary pieces of antiquity here, because for as long as Aristos had been in charge he had managed to prevent the important items from being moved to Athens for display in the National Archaeological Museum. And Aristos, now about sixty and one of the best-known faces on the island, had been here for many, many years. In fact, most of the locals simply called him 'The Curator'.

"Come in, Martin!" shouted Aristos as soon as he heard Day's footsteps on the stairs. "Have you brought me another interesting discovery?"

Day grinned at this reference to some ancient objects which he had once brought to the museum for safe keeping, and which Aristos had sent off to be examined by experts in Athens.

"No, Aristo, not unless you think I discovered something in the Mani while lecturing on fortified towers!"

"That sounds interesting. I'd like to hear about it over a nice lunch, but I'm expecting Nick Kiloziglou at any moment."

"That's fine, I just popped in to tell you some good news, and ask a favour. The good news is that Alex from the British Museum is arriving on Sunday to start work with me on a joint project. You remember Alex, don't you? The man who asked you about an artefact exchange with the British Museum…"

"Of course. Pity I couldn't help him. I liked Alex. Am I going to meet him again this time?"

"Yes, I thought we could all meet up again while he's here. I'll fix something up and let you know. Now, the favour I came to ask is that

I'd like to take a closer look at one of the *kraters* you keep in storage in the basement. Could I pop in one day after the visitors have gone, maybe on Thursday?"

Day was not sure why the *krater*, a wide-topped vessel for mixing water and wine, was not on display, unless it was because this particular one was from Cyprus rather than from Naxos. He remembered that it was beautifully painted. Day had examined it two years ago on a trawl through the museum's cellar while preparing a book on drinking vessels from the Classical period, a book he had been working on for several years with virtually no hope of ever finishing. He had suddenly realised that this *krater* might also be relevant to the book that he and Alex would be writing.

"Yes, Thursday's fine. Come here to my office first and I'll open the cellar for you myself. Bring Alex if you like."

"Good idea, thanks. So, you're expecting Nick? Has he started work on that new project of his, the tower renovation?"

"Yes, they've certainly completed the survey. He rang me this morning and said he had something to show me. He said it was exciting."

"I'll leave you to it, then," said Day, rising, but at that moment they heard footsteps on the stairs and the Australian-Greek appeared at the open door. He was flushed and had a canvas shoulder bag over his arm.

"Hi Nick,"said Day, getting to his feet and extending a hand. "I'm just on my way out."

"Tell you what, Martin, why don't you stay? You should see this too."

Nick Kiloziglou closed the office door behind him carefully as if to ensure their privacy. Despite his feelings for Nick's wife, Day could not help liking him. He had good brains, common sense and boundless enthusiasm when it came to historical buildings. Nick moved a few books off the only spare chair in the room and sat down heavily; Aristos's office was typically untidy and most of the clutter consisted of books.

"Look, I've brought something to show you, but I'll tell you the story first. My deputy Orestis and I started surveying the Di Quercia Tower, just to get an idea of the overall structure before bringing in the scaffolders. There were originally three internal floors, mostly lost now, and the superstructure has weaknesses on one side but can be saved, more or less. All the original woodwork is gone, of course. The interior walls have disintegrated, leaving just the shell of the building. The cellar, though, is in great condition due to the original vaulted ceilings. Sorry to bore you with all this, but the important thing is that the tower isn't in imminent danger of collapse, especially as there are signs that people have been in there recently. And the cellar in particular is sound.

"Orestis and I went down to take accurate measurements within the cellar. It's quite big, lots of debris, but someone has cleared a way through. We found a walled-up hiding place big enough to conceal a man and we moved some small blocks until we could see inside. I was afraid we'd find a skeleton, to be honest! But no, not a skeleton. Something almost as surprising…"

He opened his canvas bag and placed on the desk a well-used windscreen cloth, the kind that looks like chamois leather. He explained it was the only suitable thing he had found in his truck to wrap round the object. Day and Aristos leaned forward curiously.

"Go ahead and open it, Aristo," said Nick.

Aristos carefully unfolded the soft cloth and brought out a small figurine. The three men gazed at it in astonishment. It was a small statuette, the stylised image of a horse, as elegant as any real animal. It was only about four inches tall, clearly made of bronze, a greenish black the way bronze looks after centuries in the earth. Yet this little object was clean, like one of the artefacts in the cabinets of the museum downstairs.

"It's stunning," murmured Day. "Geometric period. Greek, of course. Mid-eighth century BCE. You agree, Aristo?"

"Yes. It looks authentic, although I'll have it checked. It's a votive offering, Nick, an object that would have been placed in a shrine."

The miniature horse had a narrow, almost tubular body with a high rump and long slender legs. A graceful tail, long enough to reach from the horse's back to the ground, joined the base on which the animal stood. The horse's neck was the broadest part of the little statue, suggesting a copious mane. The muzzle was extended and the ears pointed forward, suggesting the natural curiosity of a young creature.

"So you think it's genuine?" Nick asked. "How old is it, did you say?"

"Over two and a half thousand years, I'd guess," said Day quietly.

"Amazing! So how did it get in the tower?"

"That is a very good question."

They agreed that the best place for the little horse was in the museum's safe. Day took pictures on his phone before it was put away. There was no guessing how long the bronze horse had been in the Di Quercia Tower, in the Venetian equivalent of a strongbox, secure from discovery or loss, or how it came to be there. The main thing was that the horse had now found its way to safety, and to scholarship. The Greek Archaeological Service would be interested to see it, and the Curator would no doubt be making an excellent argument for keeping it on Naxos.

Nick and Aristos went to find some lunch, but Day, who had no appetite, declined their invitation and walked back to his car. He drove to the supermarket outside Chora, bought whatever took his fancy, and went home to Filoti. When he let himself in, Helen was sitting on the balcony reading a book, a small plate of cheese and olives on the table in front of her.

"Oh good, you went to the supermarket," she said, getting up to help put away the food. Day began to unpack from the carrier bags. Lemons, Feta cheese, tonic, crisps, salty nibbles, olives, tomatoes and a small but expensive bottle of Cretan olive oil.

"Martin Day, you've just bought things for gin and tonic, and a few snacks!"

"Better than not having them," he grinned, "and we'd nearly run out! Wait till you hear what's just turned up."

7

The rest of the week passed pleasantly. Helen used the Fiat most days to get to the Literary Festival. Her low spirits had been expelled by her new role and she was back to her old self, much to Day's relief.

Today, however, as she was not required at the Festival, she had gone for a quick swim at Agia Anna and Day had spent many hours reading an academic journal. It completely exhausted him and eventually he retired for a nap. He did not even hear Helen return.

He was woken after a couple of hours of deep sleep by the sound of his mobile ringing. He reached for it from the bedside table and saw the caller was Nick.

"Martin? Thank God you picked up. Bit of an emergency, mate! Are you in Filoti?"

"Yes. What's happened?"

"I've had a call from a guy in Apeiranthos who thinks there's a fire at the Di Quercia Tower. He says he can see some smoke from that direction. Look, the tower's off the road about five kilometres beyond Filoti - would you mind going to take a look? I'm at the house in Plaka, and it'll take me at least half an hour to get there. I've called the fire department in Chora, but they might need directing to the best access, there's only a grass track …"

"Sure, I'll be there in ten minutes. I'll see you when you get there."

He rang off, put on his shoes and called Helen as he searched for the car keys in the main room.

"There might be a fire at the tower Nick's restoring," he explained. "I can get there quicker than he can, so I'm going now."

"I'm coming too," she said, and stopped only to fetch her mobile before joining Day at the car.

As they drove north towards Apeiranthos, Day told Helen what Nick had said. At first they saw nothing due to the bends in the road, but in five minutes they saw the plume of white smoke that had alerted Nick's informant. Then they saw the ruined Di Quercia Tower, and the fire just beyond it.

"My God! Is the tower itself alight?"

"Can't tell. Hold on!"

Day took the rutted track to the tower at speed. The Fiat rattled and shook but didn't let him down. He braked well short of the tower and got out, phone in hand, and called 199 for the fire service. He was going to leave nothing to chance.

"I need the fire service. Martin Day. D-A-Y. The Di Quercia Tower, off the road between Filoti and Apeiranthos, nearer Apeiranthos. The fire's in the dry fields behind the tower, it's got a strong hold, I can't see if the tower's alight or not, but the fire looks as if it's spreading. They're already on the way? Good. Thank you."

He closed the phone. "They're already en route. I'm just going to take a closer look. You keep a watch out for Nick. Just a chance he might get here before the fire engine."

Without waiting for Helen's inevitable protests, Day strode off towards the tower. It was the first time he'd seen it, and he wondered if it would be the last. The scaffolding-clad structure was between himself and the fire, so he walked round it to see the extent of the blaze. As he pushed through dried grasses, spiky sedge and desiccated shrubs to the further side of the old building, he could see that the fire had been burning fiercely close to the wall but was now spreading away from the road towards the valley. The flames were being fanned by a slight breeze. The smoke was being blown away from him, but the noise of the fire was easy to hear in the comparative silence.

As Day looked on, appalled, he caught sight of a solid shape at the foot of the tower, a shape blackened by fire but from which the flames had begun to move away. His heartbeat quickened in horror and disbelief; he looked more closely. Taking out his phone, he called the police.

Nick and the police arrived at the same time, just ahead of the fire trucks. Day was pleased to see that Inspector Cristopoulos, the Chief of Police, had come in person. Day had spent quite a lot of time talking to Cristopoulos in the recent past, but surprisingly still found his presence reassuring.

Once the police had established that the fire service, which was only minutes behind them, had a clear access to the fire, and some officers had been sent to report on the blaze, Cristopoulos turned to Nick and Day without preamble.

"Which of you reported seeing a body?" Day noted that the inspector was looking directly at him. He nodded.

"I did, Inspector. I arrived here first and went to take a closer look at the fire. I'd called the Fire Department, though they were already on their way. Then I saw a shape at the foot of the tower on the other side. I hope I'm wrong, but that's what it looked like."

"A dead body."

"Very much so."

"Do you have any idea who it could be?"

"No."

"Have you seen anyone in the area since you've been here?"

Day shook his head.

"Right. Go back to your cars and be prepared to move right away if my officers or the Fire Service instruct you to. I'll need to speak to you again."

One of his men was running towards him, and the fire engines could now be seen approaching along the main road. Nick, Day and Helen stepped off the track and went back to the cars.

"What's this about a body, Martin?" asked Nick, raising his voice above the noise of the passing fire trucks.

"When I went round the back to see how far the fire had spread, I saw a long, dark shape. There was something standing up in the air from it. Frankly it looked like a body with an arm raised."

Nick's mouth opened. "God Almighty!"

Helen had heard too and turned away to get into the Fiat. Day cursed his insensitivity. She sat in the driving seat with the door open, her feet on the grass, a hand over her mouth.

"Are you all right?" he asked.

"Yes."

Day nodded, fearing to ask her anything more. He remembered another occasion and another dead body which Helen herself had discovered in a stone hut in the hills near Melanes. She had been calm then too, at the time. Day turned back to look at the blaze, shaking his head, now thinking not of the tower or its possible victim, but of Helen.

Time passed, and Nick and Day leaned against the bonnet of Nick's truck waiting for the police and watching the firemen tackle the blaze. The fire service's response was impressive: there were four fire engines and about fifteen men. It was impossible to tell from where they were if the tower itself had caught fire or whether the emergency services were beating it. It was a bad time of year for a wild fire. The land was parched by the long summer and high winds were forecast. If this got out of control, there were farms and even whole villages at risk.

At last they saw Cristopoulos, short and stocky, not built for the terrain, making his way heavily towards them. He greeted Helen, and Day introduced Nick.

"They seem to be controlling the spread of the fire, as far as I can tell," said Cristopoulos, "but it could have been extremely serious in these conditions. It was good that we caught it early. However, I fear you were right. The scene of crime team are on their way, because the object you saw is almost certainly a body. I trust you'll be available when we need to speak to you again, Martin?"

He had clearly decided to abandon the use of Day's surname, which Day noted with some surprise. There could be few civilians on Naxos better known to Inspector Cristopoulos than Day, but they had always addressed each other formally. Day did not even know the inspector's first name.

"Of course," Day said.

Nick pulled out a business card and wrote his current home address on the back. Cristopoulos couldn't bite back his reaction.

"You live on a yacht, *Kyrie* Kiloziglou?"

"Only temporarily, Inspector. We have a house in Plaka almost ready to move into."

"I see. Thank you both. I'll be in touch."

With a small nod to Helen, he walked back to his waiting police car.

Day turned to Nick. "Why don't you come back to our house, Nick? It's only six o'clock and we can give you a coffee or something before you drive to Plaka. Give you time to calm down a bit."

"Yeah, thanks, that would be good. I'll ring Deppi then follow you to your place."

They sat on the balcony with drinks, talking about what had happened. Helen was drinking tea, while Nick and Day each had a small glass of red wine. Nick looked grateful for the company.

"What do you make of it, Martin?" he said, staring across the valley without focussing. "The Di Quercia Tower is in the middle of nowhere. Could the fire really have started naturally? I'm hoping we don't have somebody who wants to stop the restoration. I suppose that poor person who died, maybe they could have started it and got into trouble."

"Wild fires usually start with a dropped cigarette, but it's not the kind of place people wander about. I really don't know. Who would want to disrupt the restoration? As for the victim, surely nobody who starts a fire stays around long enough to get caught up in it."

"It's still an amazing coincidence that the tower is set on fire as soon as you arrive to start renovating, Nick," said Helen quietly.

"We have a whole lot of questions and no chance of answers. Look, I'd better be going, I've got to pick up Deppi and Nestoras at the Plaka house and take them back to the yacht before Nestoras gets overtired. Another night on board, but hopefully not too many more of them."

"Keep in touch," said Day, as he saw Nick out. This time it was with no ulterior motive.

8

Alex Harding-Jones arrived at Athens Venizelos Airport on the following Sunday afternoon, took the Metro to the port of Piraeus and bought a one way ticket for Naxos on the ferry due to leave at five thirty. It had been a long day. His ferry, the *Blue Star Delos*, arrived at Naxos at half past eleven at night.

Day met the ferry and his surprisingly upbeat friend.

"Hey, Martin! Thanks for meeting me. It's great to be back."

"Great to see you! Journey OK? The car's over here…"

He picked up one of Alex's small bags and led the way through the port crowd towards the town, struck afresh by the beauty of the island at night. The sea and the sky were a dark foil for the scintillating lights of the town, from the street lamps and the tavernas in the foreground up to the heritage floodlights on the old walls of the Kastro. The giant portal of the unfinished Temple of Apollo at the far end of the town, the Portara, glowed magically in the darkness. The gentle rocking of the tall yachts moored along the quay beckoned in the peacefulness of the night.

The road from Chora to Filoti, however, was a different matter. There was no moon that night. The island's interior was perfectly dark with a sky full of stars, and there was no lighting along the way other than in the villages through which he drove. Day was grateful he knew the road so well. In Filoti there were still a few people in the tavernas and bars, but the village was quiet. He drove on and pulled up outside his house.

"The last time I was here, I was with Kate," mused Alex.

A picture of Alex's girlfriend, Kate Russell, sitting on the balcony of the Filoti house, came straight to Day's mind. Kate was a historian like Alex, and taught at the University of Warwick. Day thought he could hear wistfulness in his friend's voice. Warwick was a long way from London.

Further reflections were cut short by Helen appearing at the door to greet them. Within fifteen minutes they had put Alex's bags in the small room that was ready for him, and were sitting in the comfortable chairs of the living room with a bottle of local red wine, a bowl of salty Greek biscuits and nuts, and a bottle of mineral water. Although it was late, nobody was ready for the evening to end.

"How's Kate?" asked Helen.

"She's fine, hard at work in the throes of the first semester. She's still enjoying it, especially as she's teaching a course on the Masters programme this year. I saw her last weekend for the first time in several weeks."

He paused and picked up his glass, smiling at them.

" Actually, I asked her to marry me, and she accepted."

"What? Fantastic!" exclaimed Helen, and Day added his congratulations. He had felt from the start that Alex and Kate made a good pair. He topped up Alex's glass, his own and Helen's, and then proposed a toast.

"Thank you!" said Alex. "No wedding date yet, but I suspect it will be a very quiet ceremony in the Christmas vacation. No fuss."

Helen gave him a look that suggested that the kind of ceremony preferred by a forty-something historian might not quite match what a young lady lecturer had in mind. She wisely took another sip of her wine without a word.

"So, what's been happening in Naxos?" Alex looked at Helen for an answer.

"Well, you know that Martin can't keep away from trouble, Alex. He's in the middle of another drama, I'm afraid."

"Not intentionally, I assure you," protested Day, and told Alex about the fire at the Di Quercia Tower.

"How gruesome!" said Alex. "Fire is terrifying. Do they know who the body belonged to?"

"Not yet, I think. I expect the police will keep that to themselves for a while. Really, I'm not involved in anything, Helen. All I did was call the emergency services."

"We'll see," laughed Helen. "We know Martin, don't we?"

"Anyway, to change the subject, I'm looking forward to starting work on the book, Alex. We could get going tomorrow morning, if you like. It'll save us a lot of time in December, when it seems you might be busy getting married! Also, I have an interesting little puzzle for you. Take a look at this."

Day brought out his mobile and opened the photo app. He found the pictures he had taken of the bronze horse and passed the phone to Alex.

"A little bronze figurine, about four inches tall. What do you make of it?"

"Very nice. We have a couple like this in the BM, but this one is exceptionally elegant. It's a Geometric votive offering, as you know, Martin. What's the puzzle?"

"Well, right now it's in the safe at the Naxos Museum. My friend Nick Kiloziglou found it a few days ago."

"Found it? Where?"

"That's the puzzle. It was in the tower that I just told you about, where the fire started. He found a secret hiding place in the cellar which looked like part of the original structure, and this little horse was tucked inside."

"But this object is thousands of years old. How could it have got into the cellar of an Early Modern tower? Is the cellar on ancient foundations?"

"Nothing like that. Somebody must have hidden it there, at some point, which is the mystery. Isn't it a lovely little object?"

There was at least no disputing the truth of that, even if much else about the figurine was in doubt.

The following morning only Helen was up early. Leaving the others to enjoy a slow start, she crept out of the house to take a walk into the village, treat herself to a coffee, and buy some fresh milk and a newspaper.

She was soon sitting among yellow and green cushions on a blue sofa outside Café Ta Xromata, the cafe named for its bright colours, her cappuccino on the table in front of her, watching the village passing by. Greek ladies were walking at a measured pace to do their daily shopping, returning some time later with bulging carrier bags. They would greet their friends as they went, sometimes stopping for a chat. An Orthodox priest ambled along the road, the hem of his black garment almost sweeping the ground, receiving warm greetings and even the offer of an *elliniko kafes* from a local café owner. Young men on motorbikes sped noisily past on their way to work, their scooters loaded with tool boxes, lengths of wood or a workmate hitching a ride. Eventually the bus from Apeiranthos arrived, virtually empty, on its way to Chora to collect tourists for the return trip.

Helen finished her coffee and left change on the table in payment. She went to the *mikri agora*, the mini market, at the other end of the village to buy milk, then crossed to the *periptero* by the bank. The useful little kiosk sold everything from newspapers to sweets and cigarettes. The local paper, The Naxian, was displayed prominently on a board on the pavement. It was impossible to miss the headline.

Το Ναξιακό

The Naxian Newspaper

FAMOUS NOVELIST DIES IN FIRE

Naxos Police and Fire Department attended a serious blaze on Saturday afternoon at the Di Quercia Tower, an unoccupied and ruined historic building located two kilometres south of

Apeiranthos. The fire was spotted by locals and dealt with by the fire service before it could spread to the rest of the valley and neighbouring hillsides.

The Police have issued a statement that the blaze tragically claimed a victim who has been identified as English novelist Ricky Somerset, one of the guests of the Naxos Literary Festival in the Bazeos Tower. The exact circumstances of Mr Somerset's death have not yet been released.

Mr Somerset, who was recently nominated for the Winterson Prize for Fiction, had attended an event at the Festival on the morning of his death. It is not known why the writer visited the Di Quercia Tower later that day, nor whether he went there alone.

Mr Somerset's partner, who is staying in guest accommodation on the island, has been informed of the tragedy.

Kiloziglou Restoration of Syros had recently been contracted by the owner of the Di Quercia Tower, *Kyria* Maria Di Quercia, to undertake work on the building and convert it to a private residence. It is not known whether the restoration will have to be delayed or cancelled as a result of the damage caused by the fire.

Inspector Cristopoulos, Chief of Naxos Police, is leading the investigation into the tragic death of the British novelist and a possible case of arson. Anyone with information relevant to either incident is asked to get in touch with the police immediately.

She wasted little time getting back to the house.

Day and Alex stared at the paper that she put on the balcony table in front of them. Day put down his coffee cup more clumsily than usual.

"It was Ricky? RICKY?"

"You knew him, Martin?" This was Alex.

Day was speechless for once, so Helen answered for him.

"Ricky was here for the Literary Festival, as the article says. He and his husband Ben took a room in the Elias House. Anyway, not only were they Martin's guests, but Martin knew Ben quite well when they were young."

Day didn't hear Alex's response. His head was spinning with one thought after another. First, a graphic memory of the black figure in the flames with what looked like one arm raised in protest. Then the image of Ben's plump and boyish face smiling as he introduced Ricky on the beach at Paralia Votsala. He wondered why neither the police nor Ben had already called him, but he supposed there was no reason why they should.

"I have to go over there," he said, getting up. "Shit! He must be distraught."

He put his phone in his pocket, grabbed a jacket and turned down Helen's offer to go with him. The door closed noisily behind him, and they heard the Fiat's engine quickly fade to silence.

Day drove through Halki and took the road to Engares. The route to Paralia Votsala was as familiar to him as any road on the island, but never had he driven it in such desperate sadness.

He took the small road that led down to Paralia Votsala and turned left towards the Elias House at the T-junction by the sea. Only one car was parked outside the house this time, and Day hoped it was Ben's. He hadn't thought what to do if Ben was not there.

Although he had his own key, Day rang the doorbell. He heard footsteps inside and the door was opened by Ben himself. The carefree, boyish smile was gone, replaced by a strained pallor and slightly bloodshot eyes. Day said nothing as Ben mutely invited him inside.

"I came in case I could help," Day said, feeling very inadequate. "I've only just found out."

"Thanks for coming, Martin. I was making a cup of tea. Want one?"

Day nodded and followed Ben to the kitchen at the back of the house. There seemed to be nobody else in the building, the others were probably at some event at the Festival. He was grateful for the chance to talk to Ben alone.

"There's no sugar," said Ben. Day said he didn't take sugar anyway. Truth was, he rarely drank tea and only because Helen made it.

"When did you find out?" Day asked when they sat round the kitchen table. Ben leaned back, as if preparing to tell a long story.

"Yesterday morning, Sunday," said Ben. "On Saturday morning, the day it happened, I dropped Ricky off at the Bazeos Tower at ten o'clock. Usually I go back and pick him up whenever he's finished, but on Saturday Ricky told me that he and a few friends were going out somewhere and one of them would drop him home later, or he'd get a taxi. He said he'd be back about eight and that we'd go and eat at the local taverna.

"I came back here, I went for a walk and had a swim, and listened to some music. It got to nine o'clock in the evening and he still hadn't come back, so I opened a bottle of wine. There was no food in the house, and I was angry that Ricky hadn't called. Then I started to get worried that he'd had an accident or something. I rang Athina. She said she would call the hospitals and phone me if she had any news. I was to call her if Ricky turned up.

"Ricky didn't come back all night. We know now that he was already... The next morning the police came and told me. Athina had called them and given them a description of Ricky, including the chain he wore round his neck and his wedding ring with our initials on it...."

Ben couldn't go on. Day waited. Finally, Ben forced himself to continue.

"Apparently Athina had been told not to contact me. The police said that a man had died in a fire and they'd found jewellery on him that matched Ricky's. They showed me the ring and I knew it was his. He died in an old ruin miles from anywhere, they said. I just don't understand, Martin."

"I'm so sorry, Ben," said Day quietly. He watched Ben rest his face in his hands, his elbows on the table. If Athina were here, Day thought, she would know what to say now.

Ben gave a choked little laugh and rubbed his hands over his face. "The police told me not to leave the house, which would be laughable in other circumstances because there's absolutely nothing here to eat. How can I be hungry when Ricky's dead?"

Day looked blankly at the man who had once been a childhood friend, astonished at how literally he had obeyed the instruction.

"OK, that's one thing I can do," he said. "I'll go and get you something to eat. It won't help to make yourself ill. I'll be back in ten minutes."

He drove to Vasilios's taverna at the other end of the beach and bought a sandwich and a tub of salad from the chill cabinet. He added a bottle of mineral water and a carton of milk, and picked up a few sachets of sugar from a bowl on a table. He could buy more substantial food later and drop it off at the house.

Ben ate gratefully, first with a distaste born of distress and then with mechanical appetite.

"You must be thinking I'm completely heartless. It's just that I've already cried it all out. I don't have anything left. I've cried for two nights. Now it's just emptiness and silence."

Day couldn't remember a better description of violent grief.

"Would it help to talk about Ricky?"

"We met in a bar in Brighton when I was playing keys in a jazz trio. When I found out who he was, it all made sense. Even chatting me up he was a perfect talker, he was never stuck for words. He was brilliant. I mean, literally brilliant. He had so much going on in his brain that sometimes he couldn't speak or write fast enough. He wanted to do everything, try everything, live life to the full in every way.

"We've been together for four years, got married two years ago. I remember the first time I took Ricky to meet my mother…." Ben looked at Day keenly. "Do you remember my mother?"

"Of course," said Day, "Julia. Of course I remember her."

"She remembers you too, she talks about you sometimes. Anyway, she and Ricky got on quite well from the start. Ricky gave her the full Somerset charm. She couldn't fail to be won over."

"Did Julia already know …?"

"… that I'm gay? Yes. I wouldn't say she was delighted, but she accepted it. I'd moved out by the time I told her, and she didn't want to push me further away, I think."

"Is your mother in good health?"

"Yes, she's in a nursing home in Tunbridge Wells. Not far from where you and your dad lived, actually."

"You used to come to our house often, I remember."

"I remember too. They were strange times, weren't they?"

Day clumsily tried to steer the subject back to Ricky. "At least you and Ricky had a few years together and it's good that you were able to get married," he said.

Ben gave him a long look which afterwards Day was not quite able to forget. In his clear, youthful, musician's voice Ben delivered a blessing Day had not seen coming.

"Look, Martin, it wasn't your fault that your father and my mother didn't marry," he said. "You mustn't think that."

9

Before Day could reply, there was an authoritative knock at the front door of the Elias House and Day got up to answer it. He opened the door to Inspector Cristopoulos and two uniformed policemen. There were two police cars on the drive. Cristopoulos did not look very surprised to see Day.

"Hello, Martin. Could we come in please?"

"Of course," said Day, releasing the door and moving into the hall.

"I'm here to talk to Mr Lear. Is he with you?"

"Yes, we're in the kitchen."

He led the way inside. In the kitchen Ben was standing up, looking at the police as if expecting news. Day followed them into the room.

"Good morning, Mr Lear," said Cristopoulos. "Please sit down. I'd like to ask you a few more questions. First let's go through what you already told us. Yesterday you said that on Saturday you had an arrangement with Mr Somerset that, contrary to your normal routine, you would not be collecting him from the Bazeos Tower after the event. The new arrangement, you told me, was that Mr Somerset would find his own way home after spending some time with a few friends from the Festival, after which he would either get a lift from one of them, or get a taxi. Is that correct?"

"Yes," said Ben. "Exactly."

"Later that evening you became concerned that Mr Somerset had still not returned, nor had he contacted you. Is that so?"

"Yes."

"At about half past ten at night, I believe, you called Miss Athina Kalogiannis?"

"Yes, because I thought she would know what to do. She's our contact at the Festival. I thought she might know where Ricky and the others had gone."

"I see."

"I told you all this yesterday, Inspector," said Ben. Cristopoulos ignored him.

"Would you be surprised to hear," he continued, "that on Saturday morning Mr Somerset told his colleagues at the Festival that he expected you to collect him as usual at two o'clock?"

Looking quickly at Ben, Day saw a look of shock and surprise that matched his own.

"Ricky was apparently looking forward to spending the rest of the day with you, Mr Lear, according to more than one person at the

Festival. This is rather different from what you gave us to understand yesterday. What happened after the event concluded on Saturday at two o'clock is now something of a mystery. Nobody at the Festival left with Mr Somerset, and nobody had made any plans to do so. It would seem that Mr Somerset was waiting for you to arrive."

"That's not possible…."

"Perhaps you can help me to understand something else? We have an eye witness who reports seeing a car matching the description of the one you've hired arrive at the Di Quercia Tower in the middle of that afternoon. The witness saw two men get out and walk towards the tower. What would you like to tell me about that?"

Ben shook his head.

"It's in your interest to give me the truth now," pressed the inspector. "The witness was across the valley, and he saw the car quite well. He also saw just one man return to the car after a while and drive away alone. Do you have anything to say now?"

"That wasn't our car, and it wasn't Ricky and I…"

"I'll take your mobile phone, please. Thank you. I'm afraid you must come with us to the police station. My officer will accompany you to put a few clothes in a bag."

"Martin?…"

Day shook his head, trying to think.

"Just do as they say, Ben," he said, as reassuringly as he could.

Ben went upstairs to the room he had shared with Ricky, a policeman behind him, their footsteps audible from the kitchen. Day turned to Inspector Cristopoulos.

"You think Ben did this? A more gentle man I have never met! He clearly loved Ricky."

Inspector Cristopoulos drew himself up to his full height, which was not very high, and cleared his throat. Passing one hand across his face, he shook his head gently. He did not need interference from Martin Day.

"I'm not certain of anything at this stage, but I cannot ignore these conflicting accounts and the eye witness testimony. As far as we know, the victim had not visited Naxos before, therefore it seems unlikely that anyone on the island had a motive to kill him. Yet it seems he was deliberately and cold-bloodedly murdered. Ben Lear is currently our only suspect. I have no choice but to arrest him."

"Arrest?" The word stood out, starkly. Cristopoulos bowed his head fractionally.

"For the moment he's just being taken in for questioning, but I have little doubt that he will be charged," he said.

"And are you sure that Ricky's death was murder, not some terrible accident?"

"Oh yes, we have no doubt of it. Forensics have found signs of a struggle on the parapet of the Di Quercia Tower, which was accessible due to the recent erection of scaffolding by the restoration company. It strongly suggests that the victim either fell after a struggle or was pushed from the top of the tower."

"My God!"

"Then we must not forget the fire. It seems to have started either near or actually on the body, it's difficult to tell and I must wait for the pathology report. The deliberate burning of a body brings several possibilities to my mind. The fire could have been started to conceal the murder or the victim's identity, of course; but the possibility of some kind of ritual can't be dismissed. A coincidental wildfire at the scene of a violent death hardly seems likely in any case."

"My God!" repeated Day. That image flooded into his mind again, the raised arm.

He watched Ben leave with the police, his stocky figure and boyish walk reminiscent of the teenager of twenty years before, except that the young Ben would have turned round and waved a cheerful goodbye before getting into Julia's car.

10

Day watched the police vehicles disappear towards the coast road. Ben's frightened face in the window of the police car left him in no doubt that once again, despite his assertion to Helen, he had no choice but to get involved.

A text arrived which he checked before setting off. It was from Helen to say that she and Alex were walking to Taverna O Thanasis. This was not unreasonable as there was virtually no food in the house. As he drove away from Paralia Votsala he decided he was not only hungry but he wanted the company of his friends, and would join them.

Thanasis's greeting became muted once he saw Day's expression. Day sat down with Helen and Alex, and poured himself water from the bottle on the table.

"How was Ben?" Helen asked.

"Devastated, and he hadn't slept for two nights. Ricky had told Ben on Saturday that he was planning to go out with a few friends from the Festival and would find his own way home. When he wasn't back by ten o'clock, Ben called Athina. Athina got on to the police. The next morning the police told Ben that they had matched Athina's description of Ricky's ring with jewellery found on the body from the fire. Ben identified the ring."

"Poor, poor Ben!" exclaimed Helen.

"It gets worse," Day went on. "We'd better order something to eat and then I'll tell you the rest."

They ordered lightly to share: a bit of grilled chicken, tzatziki, a salad and two portions of chips. Day's need for chips at this point was self-evident.

"While Ben and I were talking in the kitchen this morning, the police arrived. It was Cristopoulos with some men, in two cars. Cristopoulos was very succinct. He said that he had statements from several people at the Festival asserting that Ricky had expected Ben to pick him up at two o'clock. Ben swears that Ricky had clearly said he would make his own way home and didn't want Ben to collect him. Then Cristopoulos talked of an eye witness, someone who saw two men arrive at the tower and only one of them leave again. The witness's account coincides with the time of Ricky's death, and the car matches the one hired by Ben and Ricky. Ben was taken to the station. I'm afraid he'll be charged with Ricky's murder."

As his friends said nothing, Day drank a whole glass of cold water.

"Do you believe Ben's side of the story, Martin?" This was from Helen, whom Day silently applauded. It was the question he had been asking himself as he drove back, and he didn't have an answer. He would give a lot to believe that Ben had told him the truth, and had nothing to do with his partner's death. Ben's innocence was going to be his working premise. At the back of his mind, tucked away, he knew that it was always a possibility, though an abhorrent one, that he was wrong.

"Yes," he told her with more conviction than he felt. "I'll work on that assumption, anyway. I'll get Ben a good solicitor, and then I'm going to find out what really happened."

He avoided Helen's eyes. He was proving her right, yet again. Let her blame him or support him, he was already involved. Without Helen saying a word, he repeated himself more firmly.

"Ben's situation is appalling, I must try to help."

She would understand much better if he were to tell her the worst thing of all, which he had no intention of sharing yet: the fact that Ricky's dead body might have been deliberately set on fire.

They ate their lunch talking lightly until most of the food was gone and Day was mechanically picking up small chips with his fork.

"I know you're not going to leave this to the police, Martin," Helen conceded, "so why don't we put our heads together?"

Day nodded gratefully and waved to the waitress to order coffee.

"Thanks. I think we should start with Ricky," he began. "Ricky told Ben one thing and a completely different thing to the other writers. Why would he do that, Helen?"

"He might have changed his plans some time in the morning and he couldn't get a message to Ben."

"Sensible suggestion," Day agreed.

"Okay," said Alex. "If Ricky changed his mind and wanted Ben to pick him up after all, he could have sent a message which didn't get through - perhaps he sent it to the wrong number, or the signal failed, or he forgot to press 'Send'. They all happen."

"Right, so we assume that for whatever reason Ben didn't know he needed to collect Ricky. Ben is still at Paralia Votsala and Ricky is stranded. How does Ricky leave the Bazeos Tower after the session? We know he did leave."

"He must have left with somebody - you can't walk anywhere from the Bazeos Tower," Helen said. This was undoubtedly true. "A taxi? Unless he hitched a lift."

"He's very unlikely to have hitched, and the police will have checked the taxis. It would seem that Ricky didn't want to contact Ben, because he could have called from the Bazeos Tower's office if he was really stuck. No, let's assume that Ricky left with somebody from the Festival. In that case there's an even more difficult question: why go to the Di Quercia Tower, of all places?"

Nobody answered for a while.

"Perhaps Ricky and the driver of the car went to the Di Quercia Tower to research it as a location for a story," suggested Alex. "That could have been what Ricky meant when he told Ben he was planning a trip with someone."

"OK, it's a deserted, semi-ruined old castle that would be an excellent place for a certain type of story, and I can easily imagine nefarious goings-on in that place!"

"You know, that could be important. Perhaps Ricky saw something he shouldn't have seen and had to be silenced?"

"Oh really, Alex, that's a bit far-fetched," said Helen. "You've been watching too many movies! This is Naxos."

Day grimaced. "Let's imagine two men from the Festival arrive at the tower. They've gone to take a look. Perhaps Ricky simply fell. He climbed to the top of the tower, to see the view perhaps, and slipped."

"And the other person just drove away? Surely anyone would try to help, stay with him, phone an ambulance? According to the witness, he drove off alone."

"I don't think we've answered the question of why Ricky told people he was being collected by Ben, when he hadn't arranged it with him," reasoned Alex. "Did he even believe it himself?"

Day rubbed his eyes; he couldn't think clearly any more. Helen put her hand on his arm.

"Have you asked Inspector Cristopoulos whether the police found Ricky's mobile phone?"

"No, I didn't, but it would have been burnt to nothing, remember."

"It's still worth asking. If it somehow escaped the fire it might answer a few questions about what happened. Oh, if only Ricky had gone home with Ben for a pleasant Saturday night in Paralia Votsala."

"I'm not sure we're getting anywhere, Martin," said Alex, finishing his coffee.

It was then that Alex showed the lateral thinking that archaeologists needed when they considered anomalies in their research.

"Let's not forget the bronze horse that was found in the same place where Ricky Somerset died," he said. "I suggest we look into that, because there's nothing normal about a two thousand year old artefact being in a three hundred year old building, the same building where a writer from Brighton mysteriously dies."

11

They spent the afternoon doing different things. Helen went for a walk to think things through and try to come up with something useful, and the men set out to discover everything they could about the little bronze horse. Their British Museum work could wait.

Leaving Alex searching the internet, Day went to his room with his laptop. Rather than start work immediately he lay on the bed and closed his eyes to think. Inevitably this resulted in falling asleep. He awoke after half an hour, feeling not guilty but refreshed, unemotional, and ablaze with a plan of action.

His first task was to call Athina. Helen had told him that Monday afternoons were left free for the Festival delegates to do what they wanted, so he thought he had a good chance of reaching her. She might already know about Ricky, but he really should have spoken to her himself before now.

"Athina? Martin here."

"Hi, Martin. Is there any news of Ricky?"

That answered his question. "So you haven't seen the local paper?"

His heart sank when she said she had not. He told her as gently as he could, omitting any reference to the image of Ricky's body which haunted him. She went silent at the other end, and then he could hear the tears and shock in her voice.

"How is poor Ben?" she managed to ask.

Day had to tell her that Ben had been taken into custody.

"Oh no! When I didn't hear anything from him, I just assumed Ricky had come back. I should have called him …"

"It's not your fault, Athina. And I should have phoned you before. Would you like to meet tomorrow? Perhaps we can think of how we can help Ben."

"Yes, please. I'm free in the morning. Why don't I pick you up at your house, so that Helen can use your car to get to the Festival? I'll drive us both there for the afternoon, when I'm working, and Helen can take you home when she finishes."

"Sounds good. What time shall I expect you?"

"I'll be there at ten. I know where you live."

She rang off, leaving Day feeling relieved. In fact, it could be very important to talk to Athina tomorrow. He hoped that Athina's knowledge of local history, in particular the history of the Di Quercia Tower, might help him to understand how the ruined building came to play such a central role in the whole thing. Somehow, he was certain, the place was important if he was to understand what really happened to Ricky.

He left his bedroom and found Helen and Alex both at the big table working on their computers. He went past them to the kitchen and poured a glass of water from the bottle in the fridge. The others hardly acknowledged his reappearance. He took his glass onto the balcony and sat facing the valley. After a few minutes he saw the mule that was often tethered in the shade of a tree in the afternoons, its work done. Nothing much was moving except for the small brown birds in his neighbour's fruit tree, and the pigeons that flirted on the reed canopy.

He let his mind settle and ideas come to him.

It was time to use his network of contacts once again. Day felt certain that the horse figurine in the Di Quercia Tower must have been stolen property. He could find no other explanation. He fetched his laptop from his room and sent an email to an art historian friend at the Sorbonne who kept his ear to the ground in the murky world of the Parisian black market. Though not, of course, dishonestly involved in the black market himself, Day's friend certainly knew a great deal about it. If anyone knew anything useful about the recent history of the little bronze horse, it might be Jacques Avian.

He sent the email and sat back to await the reply. Within a couple of minutes he was bored, and went to see how Alex was getting on.

"You'd be amazed how many of these little horse figures there are in museums around the world," Alex said. "They're all slightly different, some with shorter tails, some with prancing legs, some small and fat little things, some that don't look like horses at all. Ours is definitely one of the most beautiful. I've just started going through the websites of the major auction houses to see if I can find an old record of sale for our figurine."

Day congratulated him on the idea and went for a shower. Somehow it had got to nearly six o'clock. He turned on the iron so that it would be hot by the time he finished, and waited for the water to run warm. Taking a shower helped him to think, and on this occasion the idea came to him that the person he had to speak to was Inspector Andreas Nomikos of the Athens Police. Day had once been invited to call him 'Andreas', but was not sure that Andreas would even speak to him now, after their last argument. On the other hand, there was a good chance that if Day's call created an opportunity for Andreas to see Helen again, Andreas might overcome his animosity.

Either way, Day had to make the call. Not only was he a senior detective, but Andreas also had a connection with the international antiquities fraud police and knew a great deal about the subject. If the bronze horse was stolen property, Andreas should be involved.

Day ironed a clean shirt, dressed and closed his bedroom window to keep out the flies. In the living room he found Helen putting away her laptop, announcing she had done enough to deserve a gin and tonic. Day understood this to be a hint, if not an instruction, and set to work. He sliced a lemon and squeezed some of the juice into three glasses, wiping the piece round the rims for flavour. He half-filled the glasses with ice and gin, and opened a fresh bottle of tonic that gave a satisfying explosion of bubbles as he did so.

"Gin time, Alex. You can stop that now!" he called.

"I think I've found something!" was the reply.

"Listen to this. A bronze horse, a votive figure from the Geometric period, originating in Greece, having four jointed legs and a long tail, all of which attach to a base… sold in 1972 by a private collector in France and bought for the sum of $35,000. The purchaser was a collector in

America," Alex said, reading from his computer. He looked up. "That could easily be our horse. The photo looks practically identical."

"And you haven't found any others with the distinctive long tail attaching to the base? Sounds hopeful then. No names of the seller or purchaser, I expect?" asked Day.

"No, they're usually not declared online. The question of how it came to be in the Di Quercia Tower is the interesting one now."

"Come on, let's take a break. We could follow up with the auction house tomorrow. Too late tonight."

They took their drinks to the balcony and Alex settled into a chair like a man who felt at home. He was already shedding some of the sedentary air that he carried round with him from his apartment in Bloomsbury to the British Museum, a daily commute that did little to prevent a certain amount of weight gain and unfitness.

"I can't believe you only arrived last night, Alex," said Helen. "Cheers. Thank you for coming back to see us."

"Good heavens, the pleasure's mine! Last time I was here, things were a little stressful. This visit puts all that in the past. Cheers! I'm looking forward to seeing more of you both and working with Martin on the ceramics book."

"Oh God, I've just realised!" said Day. "I'm not going to be around tomorrow! I'm so sorry, Alex, I won't be able to start work."

If Alex was surprised he covered it well. "No problem, I'll have a go on my own. I'd have done the same thing at home anyway, and it's much more congenial here."

"Did you plan on having the car tomorrow, Martin?" said Helen. "I'm working at the Festival again. I'll need the car from eleven o'clock."

"You'll have the car all day. I'm being collected by Athina at ten. She was very upset about Ricky, we said we'd meet to talk about it. I'm also going to ask her everything she knows about the Di Quercia Tower. I think it must have a bearing on Ricky's death. After that she'll drive me to the Festival in time for the afternoon event and I'll come home with you when you finish."

It was only hours later, when they said goodnight and each went to their room, that Day checked his emails. Jacques Avian had replied. He sounded more than a little pleased with himself.

Martin,

Good to hear you're still alive and kicking. Greece must be good for you. You gave me an interesting challenge with your question about the bronze horse with the long tail. As it happens, it's quite well known in certain circles, and I can tell you a little about it.

It was bought in the 1970s at auction for over $30,000 by an American collector who later retired to the Peloponnese. Just under two years ago it was stolen during a daring and highly successful robbery. The property was thought to be completely secure, but the thieves got away with many valuable antiquities, some of them so rare as to be priceless. The house was somewhere in the Taygetus Mountains, I think. The American collector, who must now be in his nineties if he's still alive, offered a reward for information about the robbery, but astonishingly (given the size of the reward) no such information was ever forthcoming. One or two items have been recovered by international police forces, a tiny fraction of the haul. It's assumed that the thieves are hanging on to the artefacts until it's safer to sell, if that's ever possible. There has been no sign of your little horse until now. I expect the reason is that it's particularly easy to identify, in fact I'd say unique. I must warn you, Martin, to be very careful. I've heard these are dangerous people.

Yours ever,
Jacques

A smile crept over Day's face as he closed the email. Good for Jacques! Now he knew exactly what he would do next. He would speak to the man Helen had once called the Viking Policeman, a Greek police inspector with Norwegian ancestry on his mother's side, fair hair and light blue eyes. Andreas Nomikos.

12

Day hesitated before he called Andreas's private number, especially this late. He was resolved to make the call, but he anticipated a gruff reception. Andreas had been in charge before when Day had involved himself in a police matter. Although it was unusual for a policeman to condone the participation of a civilian, Andreas recognised that Day had his uses and could achieve things that the police could not. The arrangement had so far worked well up to the point where Day overstepped the mark. It was something he had done on more than one occasion.

The last time he had seen Andreas, the policeman had called Day a liability and, most hurtful of all, said that he had been wrong to trust him. Day had lost his temper and driven away at some speed. They had not met again.

He brought up the phone number and allowed his index finger to hesitate above the call button for a second.

"*Oriste*," said Andreas at the other end.

"*Kalispera*, Andrea. It's Martin Day."

There was a fractional pause during which Day imagined that Nomikos was recalling their last encounter, remembering his brief relationship with Helen, and wondering about the reason for Day's call.

"*Kalispera*, Martin. Is Helen all right?"

Clearly Andreas could imagine no reason why Day should call him other than to give him bad news about the woman he found extremely attractive. Day knew there was only one way to proceed.

"Helen's fine, and I'm sorry to call rather late. I'm phoning to apologise to you, Andrea. For last time we met. You had every right to be angry. I couldn't see it then but I understand now, and I hope we can move on."

Again, Andreas did not respond at once. Day took nothing for granted, for Andreas was a most unusual and unpredictable man. Moreover, Day really had given him every reason to be annoyed.

"I hear you. I don't believe in holding on to anger, and for two intelligent men to fall out over an error would be a pity. Very well, your apology is accepted. Was there any other reason for your call?"

"Yes, I have some information for you. You'll be interested to hear about this because it concerns the theft of antiquities."

"Go on."

"I've recovered a very distinctive Greek figurine which was stolen in a robbery about two years ago and has not been seen since. It's a small bronze horse made in the Geometric period."

"How do you know this about the robbery, Martin?"

"I know someone in Paris, an art history specialist who was at university with me. He keeps his finger on the pulse of the covert market in antiquities. He recognised the photograph of the figurine and knew about the robbery."

"How did you come by the figurine?"

"It was found during the early stages of a building restoration on Naxos by the restorer, another friend of mine called Nick Kiloziglou."

"I see. Where is it now?"

"In the safe of the Naxos Archaeological Museum."

"Good. Can you send me all the details you have, and photos of the figurine?"

"I can and I will. There's more, Andrea."

Andreas Nomikos grunted slightly as if vindicated in some apprehension. Day didn't wait to be asked.

"It concerns the building in which the object was found, a ruined Venetian structure in the heart of the island, called the Di Quercia Tower. Some days after the bronze horse was found, there was a fire and a man died. The Naxos police are certain it was murder, that the victim was pushed from the parapet."

"Is there a known connection between the victim and the artefact?"

"No. The victim was an English novelist who was visiting Naxos for the Literary Festival. There's also no clear reason for him to have been anywhere near the tower."

"And nothing else was found with the bronze horse?"

"Nothing. It was in an old hiding place in the cellar, and nothing else was in there. The robbery apparently took place at a private residence in the Peloponnese belonging to an old American collector - do you happen to know about the case?"

Day heard the interest ignite in Andreas Nomikos.

"I most certainly do. I was connected to the team that investigated it about two years ago. Very little of what was stolen has ever been recovered, and no evidence has emerged that could be used against the suspects. Not only that, but they've gone to ground and no more robberies have taken place that we believe were committed by them."

"What do you want me to do?"

"You? Nothing! I'll come to Naxos in the next day or so and speak to my colleague Cristopoulos. He'll remain in charge of the murder investigation, but I want to follow up on the robbery. I don't like unsolved antiquities crime, as you know, Martin." He paused briefly. "Shall I see you and Helen?"

"If you'd like to. We'd love to see you."

Even as he spoke Day realised his reply sounded stilted, and with good reason. Helen might refuse to see Andreas. He hoped Andreas had not noticed, despite his good grasp of English.

"Then I shall look forward to it. Goodbye for now."

13

"So where are you taking me?" Day laughed.

Athina Kalogiannis was a confident driver, as she was confident in everything else. There was no sign now of the emotions of the day before. She drove the convertible Suzuki Jimny from Filoti to Halki in less time than Day thought possible. He found he was rather enjoying himself.

"We're nearly there. It's a small bar I know in Halki. I think you'll like it. There's a special reason that I've chosen this particular place, you'll find out after we arrive."

Day resigned himself to waiting. They parked at the side of the main road and Athina locked her car with an air of abandoning it to its fate. Day would have driven an extra half mile to the public car park, chosen a spot in the shade and locked the car with care. With a flourish of her arm, Athina deposited the car keys in her bag, swung it over her shoulder and led Day into the centre of the village.

Halki was once thought of as the island's capital, but its pedestrianised centre was compact and relatively small. Compressed into this area were many delights: several attractive places to eat, a famous marble art boutique, a photography gallery, the island's museum of Kitron liqueur, and a shop containing a large loom on which someone was usually demonstrating the traditional craft of weaving. Day always enjoyed visiting Halki, and wondered which of the cafés Athina had chosen.

She led him past several excellent places with attractive outdoor tables where Day would have been delighted to stop. They continued to walk along narrow lanes in which the cement around the flagstones had been painted white and the ground was spotlessly swept. The buildings were either whitewashed or left unpainted with the render showing its age, which was attractive in this setting. Here and there a bougainvillea grew bravely from a small hole in the lane, its thin, bare stems reaching skyward until it opened like a parasol over the street in fiercely luminescent red flowers.

Athina stopped at a modest bar with only a handful of tables outside. It was a place Day had not visited before, barely as wide as a single room. The outdoor chairs and tables were red, and when she sat down at a small, round table in her red blouse and white trousers, Athina looked as if she belonged there.

"Come and sit next to me, Martin *mou*," she said, indicating the chair next to hers.

They sat facing the open door of the bar, which was invitingly shaded by a red awning and flanked by an A-frame blackboard advertising Mythos beer on which someone had chalked the daily specialities. Day noticed the name of the bar, *To Mavro Velanidi*.

"*Velanidi*. That's not a word I know. What does it mean?"

"Bravo, Martin *mou*!" laughed Athina. "The name of the bar is one of the things I wanted you to notice. It means The Black Acorn. Now you have five minutes to work out why I brought you here."

A large Greek with wild black hair, laughing dark eyes and a big beard stepped out of the bar and came to their table. He was wearing a sand-coloured apron with an air of pride.

"*Kalimera Kyrie, Kyria.* What can I get you? Would you like to see the menu?"

"No, just coffee please," said Athina. "I'd like a frappé."

Day, who always drank frappé on a warm day, ordered the same and received a look from Athina as if somehow he had paid her a compliment.

"Right away," said the proprietor, and returned to his bar. A young girl with a tray then arrived and placed two glasses of iced water, a bowl of sugar lumps, and a tumbler containing their rolled-up bill on the table.

"So, have you worked it out?" said Athina.

"No. I haven't a clue, but I like this bar. Why are we here, other than to have coffee?"

"You see, I know why you wanted to talk to me, Martin. You want to find out what happened to Ricky, but you need some help. Am I right?"

Day sighed and gave a small laugh. "Why would I want more than the pleasure of your company, Athina?" he said. "But you're right."

"I want to help Ben and help you find out what happened to poor Ricky. You need to know why he went to the Di Quercia Tower? I can tell you about it."

The proprietor appeared with their coffee which gave Day a moment to cover his surprise. As he placed the glasses on the table he stepped back and looked at Athina with a frank but courteous smile.

"Don't we know each other, *Kyria*? I seem to remember that you brought groups of visitors here in the summer."

"You're quite right! I'm a tour guide for the Tourist Office. My name is Athina Kalogiannis, this is my friend, Martin Day."

"Kostas Artsanos," said the man, shaking hands. "*Kalos Irthatay*! Welcome!"

"How is your wife Anna? I met her a few times over the summer."

"Anna is very well. I'll tell her you were here. She's shopping in Chora."

Kostas Artsanos gave a small bow and went back into the bar. A few minutes later he returned carrying a plate on which were two slices of homemade cake and a few spoon sweets, which he gave them as a gift.

"I hope you have a sweet tooth," murmured Day when Kostas Artsanos had gone, "because I don't like cake and we don't want to offend your new friend."

"Mmm. I may have to do the polite thing," Athina said, breaking off a piece of marbled sponge. "Poor you, this is delicious!"

"You're going to have to tell me why you chose this place. I give in."

"Ah, your deductive powers are asleep, I see. The name of the bar is a joke that Kostas is making against himself. He's quite round and his hair is black: the black acorn is meant to be Kostas himself. There are two more important things to know about Kostas and his bar. Can you see a connection between the bar and the Di Quercia Tower, now that you know about the acorn?"

Day held up his hand to stop her while he waited for his brain to work. "Quercus is an oak tree, right? Acorn and oak tree."

"You've got it. Di Quercia is the name of the Italian family who now own the tower, and the name means 'made of oak' in Italian. It's a modern corruption of an old Venetian family name. The tower was originally built by a Venetian family who lived on Naxos. Many generations ago there was a family feud and part of the family left Naxos and went back to Italy, where they flourished and became extremely wealthy. The tower, which has stood empty for many years, is now to be restored by their descendants as the family home in Greece."

"Interesting!" said Day. "What's the link between this rich Italian family and our friend Kostas, the black acorn?"

"I see your brain has woken up, *agapi mou*. After the feud, the poorer members of the family, who remained on Naxos, became known by the name Velanidia, which is an old Greek word for oak. The proud Velanidias had no family home, and only their name to show for their lineage. The family dwindled until finally even the name died out, with no male heirs to carry it on. The last child, a baby girl, married a man who, contrary to Greek custom, insisted she drop her family name and use his only - Artsanos. That girl was Kostas's mother."

"So, there are no more Velanidias on Naxos. Do you think Kostas deliberately named his bar The Black Acorn to show his connection to the old Velanidia family?"

"Possibly. I don't know how much he and Anna know about the history."

"Well, you've certainly done your homework. I'm impressed."

"I love delving into the history of Naxos, Martin. If I don't know something, I have to find out."

"Do you know if Kostas's branch of the family ever lived in the tower?"

"I don't think so. The Velanidias lived in Sifones until The Departure."

"Sorry, I don't follow."

"Haven't you heard of Sifones? It's a village between Kinidaros and Moni, not very far from the Di Quercia Tower, but it's not there any more. I mean, the houses are still standing, but nobody lives in them. 'The Departure' is what people call the time when everyone abandoned Sifones. I don't know for certain what happened, but there are many exaggerated local tales that fascinate the tourists!"

"Do you know where the people of Sifones went to after leaving the village? Particularly the Velanidia or Artsanos family?"

She shook her head and pushed her hair back from her face.

"Most people settled in one of the larger villages in the area. I'm fairly sure most of the older members of the family are dead now. Kostas made enough money working in the bars in Chora to buy this bar and marry his very nice wife. Thanks to talking with Anna, I found out that Kostas has a brother and a sister. The sister got married and now lives in Apeiranthos. I think the other brother became a sheep farmer, but they seem to have had a falling out with him."

"You're a fountain of knowledge, Athina. What can you tell me about the Di Quercia Tower itself? How long has it been empty?"

"Since the rich family left for Italy generations ago."

"Was it closed off?"

"I don't know. I doubt it. Who would have done that in those days?"

Day nodded. He wondered how many of the stone blocks that had once been part of the Di Quercia Tower had been carried away and used in the construction of nearby walls and barns.

"So anybody could get into the tower at any time?"

"Yes. But why would anyone want to? Unless for a 'romantic rendezvous' perhaps…"

Athina gave him a meaningful smile and helped herself to a spoon sweet that looked as if it had once been a piece of kitron fruit. The syrup on her spoon was a sticky gold substance that she seemed to find delicious. She licked her fingers carefully and dried them on a paper serviette. Having finished, she turned to him with a conspiratorial flourish.

"Now let's talk about the Festival a little, Martin *mou*. Would you like to guess the name of a very influential lady who has sponsored the Festival and who will be arriving in a few days' time?"

"No," he sighed. "Please just tell me!"

"Signora Maria Di Quercia!"

"The owner of the tower?"

"That's right. I'll introduce you to her. Also, you must talk to my hospitality manager, Adonis Galanis."

Day waited but was eventually forced to ask.

"Why?"

Athina brought out her answer with considerable pride.

"He's married to another oak sapling, Kostas's little sister. You can talk to him and carry on your investigations into the former Velanidia family."

Athina parked at the side of the Bazeos Tower where other cars were already soaking up the heat of the cheerful October sun. She pulled on the hand brake, sighed loudly and turned to Day.

"I enjoyed spending the morning with you, Martin *mou*. What a pity it's come to an end. What are you doing this evening? I could cook some dinner for us at my apartment? You will come, won't you?"

Day was tempted. Not only was he tempted, but he needed to avoid offending Athina.

"I'd love to, but I have a friend from England staying with me," he said truthfully. "Could we make it next week?"

"All right, but I won't let you say no to me next week! Let's go in, you can sit by me. I think you'll enjoy yourself."

The main room was packed with book-lovers of many nationalities. As Writer in Residence, Helen was hosting a conversation session with Corky Armitage, the Irish doyenne of crime fiction. Helen spoke knowledgeably about Corky's books, and skilfully led the old lady through the story of her life from when she was a naïve young writer to her current elevated position. Day was impressed. He had never heard Helen speak in public before, not even when they were both teachers in London years ago. He was used to talking endlessly about the subjects he loved, and it gave him a strange and unexpected pleasure to watch Helen do the same.

He became aware of Athina slipping into the aisle seat next to him and noted the proximity of her shoulder. When the talk ended she walked to the platform to thank the speakers on behalf of the audience and invite everyone to enjoy refreshments in the courtyard.

Helen was clearly much in demand. Day managed to find a brief moment of privacy to congratulate her before Athina joined them with a young man in tow who carried a tray of glasses and had been offering them to the guests.

"Martin, Helen, what will you have to drink? Wine or juice? By the way, may I introduce my excellent head of hospitality, Adonis Galanis? Adoni, you must find time to talk with Martin, who is interested in the history of Sifones. I'm sure you can tell him far more than I can."

The young Greek nodded politely, facing Day fully for the first time. Adonis by name, thought Day, Adonis by nature. God's gifts were certainly not evenly distributed in this life. He glanced at Helen and saw that his own assessment of the young man's astonishing good looks was not exaggerated. Helen caught his expression and began to laugh, which she covered by accepting a glass of wine and raising it to Athina.

"Well done, Athina, that went well, I think."

With a polite excuse, Adonis Galanis moved away to offer drinks to the small groups of guests who stood around the courtyard. As Athina and Helen chatted, Day had a chance to look round at the other people and at the wonderful setting. The courtyard in front of the tower was an ideal venue for such a reception: it was spacious, its gravel floor meticulously swept, and rising above it the sheer stone walls of the tower were imposing. The front facade was crowned with a small bell tower and a high parapet from which the Venetian landowner would have surveyed his domain. Day had been to events here at night, when the tower walls were floodlit with a soft amber glow that transformed the courtyard into something even more magical.

Athina leaned in to Day and lowered her voice to a whisper. Helen could hear every word, but was clearly not included in this conversation.

"Martin, why don't you come here to see me tomorrow, and I'll make sure you have an opportunity to speak to Adonis about you-know-what? We could go to lunch together afterwards?"

"As I said, I'm afraid I can't tomorrow, another time maybe. Is there a particular reason why I should talk to him?"

"It's only a feeling. I saw him talking to poor Ricky several times, and he knows about the Artsanos family and the old tower."

"I see." This wasn't true, he felt none the wiser, but he said it anyway.

"I've remembered something about the other Artsanos boy, Kostas's older brother," went on Athina in a low voice. "His name was Sotiris. He and Kostas were both much older than their sister, and Sotiris moved to an old farm near Sifones after The Departure, though I've heard he wasn't a very good farmer. He and Kostas apparently had a big falling out many years ago."

With that Athina excused herself, gave Day and Helen the customary kiss on both cheeks and disappeared into the building. Not long after finishing their drinks, they quietly slipped away themselves.

"That young lady is after you, Martin Day!" said Helen when they were driving home in the Fiat.

"It's not like that. Athina is very personable with everybody, from the delegates to the bar staff."

"Personable? Well, by all means go where she's leading if that's what you want, but if a full-blown relationship with her isn't what you're looking for, just be aware that's what she has in mind."

Day was increasingly focussing on his forthcoming siesta, so rather than argue he simply thanked Helen for her observation.

14

Alex closed his laptop with an air of finality. Having now spent a day and a half working together on the basic structure of the book for the BM, he and Day had done as much as they could for the time being.

"Well, that's that for now. We can work separately until you come to London in December."

"I think it's looking promising. Why don't we take a break and get out of the house? Do you fancy a trip to Chora? I'm due to meet Aristos Iraklidis, the museum curator, to look at a particular pot in his storage cellar. He'd like to meet you again, and the pot may interest you. Want to come? I'd value your opinion. I've not seen it for several years, but it's a *krater* with horse and chariot motif; I think it's very similar to one in the BM."

"That could be important. Yes, I'll come with pleasure."

They arrived in the foyer of the Naxos Museum several minutes before closing time. Aristos came down from his office to take them into the vast cellar beneath the building where the museum kept partial items, sherds and damaged objects. There were also a few things, like the item that Day wanted to see again, which were in good condition but for some reason not put on display.

Aristos greeted them both and led them through to the back of the museum. The public were not allowed in this part of the building, and Day loved the feeling of privilege that always flooded him when he came here. Aristos unlocked a sturdy door down to the cellar. Switching on lights and consulting the paper in his hand for the location of the object, he was like a monk exploring a crypt.

"So you want to see the Cypriot Chariot Krater, Martin. May I ask why?"

"It's to do with the book that Alex and I are preparing. I saw the *krater* here a couple of years ago and it came to mind when I handled one in the BM last year, the one called the Larnaca Krater. They're both decorated with chariots pulled by pairs of horses, and the shape is similar. I was just curious to take another look."

"You think they might be by the same painter? You say the *krater* in the British Museum came from Larnaca originally?"

"Yes. And your *krater* is also from Cyprus."

"Interesting. That reminds me, have you found out anything more about the little bronze horse?"

"Yes. Alex went onto an auction house website and learned that it was bought in 1972 by a collector in America. We then discovered that it was stolen a couple of years ago in a major robbery in the Peloponnese and hasn't been seen till now. We still don't have any idea how it came to be in the Di Quercia Tower."

They were now deep in the storage cellar beneath the museum. It was a labyrinth of floor-to-ceiling shelving in a damp, ill-lit vault that smelled of dust, clay and age. On the lower shelves were large tins on which a twentieth-century coffee manufacturer's logo was still visible, each one overflowing with pottery sherds found on Naxos over the years and still awaiting examination. There were so many that it was impossible to imagine the job ever being completed.

Aristos found the shelf he was looking for and lifted down a large, rounded clay vessel on a narrow base. It was about thirty centimetres high, had a wide opening at the top and small handles attached at the rim and the shoulder on either side. One of the handles was broken, and a small piece was missing from the rim, but otherwise the vessel seemed to be in good condition. It had clearly suffered damage in the past but been well repaired. It was decorated with pairs of proud horses drawing chariots driven by warriors shown in profile. Between the chariots were abstract decorations shaped like palm leaves. Typical of the period, the pair of horses that pulled each chariot were indicated by a single horse's body with eight legs and two heads. A similar technique was used to suggest the chariots and the warriors.

Day took it carefully from Aristos and enjoyed the weight of it in his hands.

"Is this what you wanted to see, Martin? The lighting's better in the examination room, or you can take it upstairs."

Day looked at the object more closely and reconsidered his first impression of its condition; it had been skilfully repaired but there was considerable damage. "It looks like this was found in many pieces, and some small bits are missing. It's still a lovely thing. But I think I'm wrong, you know. I don't think it bears any significant resemblance to the one in the British Museum after all. My memory has let me down. I was so sure, too."

"Don't let it bother you, Martin," said Alex. "The memory plays tricks. There are similarities between this and the Larnaca Krater, but this one is not quite as carefully painted. Look, the details on the wheel there are quite badly drawn."

Nodding, Day gave the vessel back to Aristos who replaced it on the shelf.

As they emerged from the cellar Day asked Aristos if he could pick his brains.

"It's local knowledge I'm after. I went to a bar in Halki called The Black Acorn, the owner is a Kostas Artsanos. I want to find out more about that family."

"Everyone knows Kostas. He has a good reputation," said Aristos carefully. "He's worked hard to build up that place. The bar's name is a reference to the fact that his ancestors used to be part of the rich old Di Quercia clan, but they were the black sheep of the family, hence the name of the bar - together with a joke about Kostas's appearance. Poor old Kostas, he didn't think about what folk say about black acorns. Have you heard this? They say they're the result of the parent tree being diseased or traumatised, and that black acorns are infertile. There's botanic evidence for it, actually. Luckily, Kostas is a good man and nobody holds it against him or his excellent little bar. If you ask around, though, people will tell you that Kostas and Anna haven't been blessed with children. Why do you ask?"

"I'm interested in the Di Quercia Tower, and clearly it was connected to this family. I'm trying to work out what happened to Ricky Somerset, of course. Do you know anything about Kostas's siblings?"

"There's a sister. She was always a pretty child, I believe she's married now. I think her name was Evangelia. Then there was an older brother who was a bit wild and I don't think he lives on the island any more.

That's all I know." Aristos shook his head sadly. "I read in the paper that Ricky Somerset's partner is being held by the police."

"Sadly true. The police don't have very much else to go on."

"The name Ricky Somerset rings a bell, I just haven't been able to remember why," murmured Aristos vaguely.

"I expect it's something to do with his books?"

"No, I'm sure it's to do with Naxos."

"I don't think so, he and Ben have never been here before."

"I see. Well, it's just another example of unreliable memory, no doubt. You're not the only one, Martin."

By the time they left the museum there were no remaining visitors and most of the staff had gone home. They said goodbye to Aristos and walked towards the port where Day had parked the Fiat. It would soon be dusk, which fell early in the Cyclades; time for aperitifs on the balcony and a fish dinner at Agia Anna. It was Alex's last night on Naxos.

Before they reached the port, Day's mobile emitted the sound that announced a text message. He stopped to read it and summarised it for Alex with relief.

"It's from Ben. He's been released without charge, and the police have taken him back to the Elias House. He can't make arrangements for Ricky's body to be taken home until the police give him permission, so he needs to extend his use of the room. I'll just send a reply."

Willingly agreeing to Ben's request, Day offered his help at any time and said he would be in touch soon. After he sent the message he noticed a new one arrive, from Andreas. It was brief and succinct. He relayed the contents to Alex.

"You remember Andreas Nomikos, the police inspector from Athens? He does some work on antiquities fraud, so I told him about the bronze horse. He's arriving tomorrow to see it. I suppose that's good."

"That's very good. You can hand the whole thing over to the police, don't you think?"

"You're sounding very like Helen," remarked Day, and refrained from saying anything else. His decision to become involved was already made. Even Helen knew that, he thought.

The lady in question appeared rested and ready for the evening when they reached the house in Filoti. Day headed straight for the shower, where he attempted to wash away the chagrin he felt at his error with the *krater*. By the time he emerged, wearing a smart shirt which he had once rashly acquired on a rare visit to a rather expensive purveyor of menswear in central London, he felt considerably better. There really was nothing as restorative as the feel of good cotton and the anticipation of a properly prepared gin and tonic.

Seeing Helen and Alex were already chatting on the balcony, he went straight to the galley kitchen and began to cut a lemon. He found the ceremony of making the drink almost as pleasurable as the end result.

"Gin, anyone?" he said, carrying them to the balcony.

"Absolutely! This is idyllic. What a shame Kate isn't here, I know she'd love to be. We'll come and see you next summer without fail."

"You're welcome any time," said Day, preparing to take his first sip. "What a shame you're going so soon, Alex, but it's been very good to see you. Where would you like to eat tonight?"

"We said Agia Anna, didn't we? Either the place you recommended before, or somewhere near there, where they do good seafood…"

"Naxos is wonderful for seafood," agreed Helen. "I've even started to buy the fresh fish from the boats to cook at home. Do you and Kate cook together?"

"Not really, because we're so rarely in the same place. Hopefully that will change after we're married."

"How are you going to work it, with you in London and Kate in Warwick? Is one of you going to change job?"

"We don't plan to yet. Frankly I'm not sure quite how things will work next year. Kate will go back in January for the new university term, and we'll have to see each other at weekends again, I suppose. Between ourselves, I'm not sure how romantic that sounds to me, at my age! We both love our jobs, though, and Kate is on a rising curve heading towards a promotion. We'll be fine. It might just be a bit strange for a while - or rather, not much different from how we live now."

Helen considered. "Well, since you're happy together now, why won't you continue to be? Over time things will evolve and you'll make changes."

"So wise, Helen. I'll drink to that. I hope I'm not too old to change my ways by then. Only joking."

Day wondered how much in fact his friend was joking, and how much making light of a real concern. Alex was about ten years older than Kate, but he was a man who was somehow older than his years. Kate was the opposite: early thirties and still full of the lightness of her youth. Perhaps, on the metaphorical eve of his wedding, Alex was having second thoughts.

"Having second thoughts, Alex?" he joked at once. In for a penny.

"What? No, not at all. I just don't want to spoil what we have. It's nonsense, of course."

"I'm sure it is, Alex," Helen said, and put her hand on his arm lightly. "Bridegroom's nerves, that's all. You and Kate have so much in common, and from what I saw you have a very easy, relaxed relationship. You just need to trust it. Excuse me a minute, I'll bring out some olives."

She left the balcony with a swing in her walk that left Day with the distinct impression that Alex's visit had finally dispelled the low spirits that had followed the completion of her last novel. That, and the work she was doing at the Festival, had helped her to return to her usual philosophical self. She was looking good too, wearing loose white trousers and a long-sleeved top which suited her very well. The colour reminded Day of the Aegean in one of its more thoughtful moods.

"I should book a taxi to take me to the ferry tomorrow morning, Martin. Do you have one you use regularly?"

"No need, we'll take you. You're on the 11:10 ferry to Rafina, aren't you? Actually I think Andreas must be arriving on that boat, so we'll see you safely on your way and then I might see if I can catch him for a quick word."

They spent another half hour on the balcony as the valley darkened and they saw the lights come on in the two distant houses that lay just within their view. Soon they noticed the stars, which one by one became faintly visible, like tiny drops of rain landing from a clear summer sky.

At Agia Anna, their favourite beach resort on the south-west coast of the island, tavernas lined the beach. Only a strip of boardwalk and the sand itself separated the restaurant terraces from the water's edge. They sauntered along the boardwalk making their choice. Some places were traditional, their tables draped with paper covers, their awnings hung with fairy lights, otherwise brightly lit. One or two were ultra modern, trendy bars with black and white decor and a long cocktail menu. It was hard not to go to their usual taverna where they knew the seafood was excellent, but instead they chose a busy restaurant where an empty table right on the edge of the terrace offered cooler air from the sea and the delicious aroma of cooking.

It must have been the most popular taverna in Agia Anna. Nearly every other table was occupied, almost exclusively by Greeks. Day felt a rush of contentment.

"I've heard about this place," he recalled. "I think they have their own fishing boat and catch the fish themselves. That is, probably some of their family members do. I'm not sure about this time of year, though."

A young woman came to the table, greeted them courteously and spread another layer of paper cover on their table, deftly clipping the edges down with metal clips. She managed this while still holding a bottle of mineral water and a bread basket which held cutlery tightly wrapped in paper serviettes with three small glasses lodged among the bread, ready to be set before them. She looked as if she did this many times every day.

"*Kalispera sas,*" she said. "I will bring you the menus in one minute. Would you like some wine?"

"A litre of white, please," said Day, making a snap decision, and was just in time. The girl had already returned to the kitchen.

"How different is this from old Thanasis's place?" said Alex, but his tone was happy. "Now, this evening is my treat, to thank you for having me. It's been wonderful."

Before they could reply the menus appeared, a jug of cold white wine and more glasses. Day poured wine for them all, and tucked into a piece of bread as he studied the menu.

"I'd like the crispy fried squid," said Helen. "I don't care if they've been frozen, it's still one of my favourites."

"In Greece there's an asterisk that tells you that the fish has been frozen," Day said in answer to Alex's questioning look. "I'm not sure but I think it's the law. Anyway, squid looks good. Come on, Alex, it's your last night, what would you like?"

"We're sharing as usual, right? How about some little fish, the deep-fried kind?"

"Agreed, here they are. *Maridia*, what we call whitebait. Salad? Chips? Both?"

They ordered, and added a warm dish of pasta with octopus, as the night was becoming quite cool. The addition of pasta did not deter Day from ordering the portion of chips. By the time the food came, Helen had covered her shoulders with a light pashmina, but the evening was still and it was perfectly pleasant to eat outside. The sea was invisible in the darkness except for the white froth where the tiny waves folded onto the sand, and where a mirror image of creamy light reflected the lights of the tavernas and bars along the shore.

They ate joyously, talking of life in London and Alex's plans to spend the next weekend with Kate. They avoided anything to do with mysteries and fires. Day's mind was pleasantly free of concern as he enjoyed the seafood, until the point at which they had cleared most of the dishes and he was pouring the last of the wine into their glasses. It was Alex who reminded him.

"I've been giving some thought to Ricky," Alex began, sitting back and shrugging apologetically. "Before I go I wanted to tell you what I think because I feel I should. I think you need to prepare yourself, Martin. Whichever way I look at it, I come back to Ricky's partner. Sometimes the most obvious answer is the right one, you know. I understand you were childhood friends, but remember the facts. Apart from Ben's own statement, everything points to his having killed Ricky - maybe accidentally, but it really could have been him. I think he may have collected Ricky from the Festival and rather than go back to the Elias House they drove to the Di Quercia Tower, climbed it, Ricky fell. The fire was started to conceal the evidence. He drove away. It's actually very plausible."

Day sniffed, putting down his glass.

"Yes, it's plausible, but it's not what happened."

"Alex is only putting a reasonable scenario to us…"

"Yes, Helen. I appreciate what you're saying, Alex. I'll keep it in mind."

15

The big *Blue Star* ferry approached the island, executed its turn in the harbour and reversed into the port. Without delay the seamen lowered the heavy vehicle ramp, which scraped noisily back and forward on the concrete of the jetty with the gentle movement of the ship until the men had secured the vessel. The policeman on duty blew his whistle a great many times, issuing instructions to passengers and vehicles which few managed to interpret. Everyone was in a hurry, not least the ferry itself, which was on a tight schedule. The passengers who wanted to embark, Alex included, were ushered aboard at the same time as those descending made their way to dry land. It seemed chaotic, but was nothing unusual in the Cyclades and everyone managed to remain good-natured.

Andreas was easy to pick out from the crowd of arriving foot passengers. He was not in uniform; it was his blonde hair which singled him out, because by mid October most visitors had gone and the passengers were mostly Greeks.

When Andreas got close to them his gaze fixed on Helen and he came towards them with a broad smile. To Day's surprise, Helen seemed delighted to see him.

"Helen, Martin, good to see you!" he said, and kissed Helen warmly on both cheeks before shaking hands with Day. "I'm surprised to see you at the port. Is this just my good luck?"

"A friend of ours has just left on your ferry," explained Day. "Do you have time for coffee with us?"

"Certainly. You can tell me about your little bronze figure, Martin, while I have the pleasure of your company." The last comment seemed to have been directed towards Helen. "I have something to tell you, too, that I think you'll find interesting."

Day suggested a good café near the police station, one which had become a favourite with him. The owner, Katerina, spotted him at once as they sat down, and arrived at their table with the usual glasses of iced water and a big smile.

"Are you expecting the Curator?" she asked him hopefully. She associated Day with her most highly respected local customer, Aristos. Her face fell slightly when Day shook his head.

"Not today, I'm afraid, Katerina. Could we have a frappé and a double cappuccino, please, and what for you, Andrea?"

"Greek coffee *sketo*, please," said Andreas, who preferred his Greek coffee unsweetened.

Smalltalk filled the time agreeably until their coffees arrived. Helen's part in the Literary Festival and the completion of her latest novel were easy subjects of conversation, and they steered clear of police business. Day looked carefully at Andreas and Helen when it was clear that neither of them were paying him any attention. Undoubtedly nothing had diminished the inspector's regard for Helen, and she was not discouraging him. Day sighed.

When he could tear himself away from his focus on Helen, Andreas asked Day to tell him more about the bronze horse.

"I told you everything I know, Andrea, and you probably know more than I do anyway. Apparently the collector from whom it was stolen offered a reward for information leading to the recovery of his antiquities, but nobody came forward. Is that still true?"

"Yes, quite true. I hope you're not thinking of claiming the reward, Martin…"

Day felt himself flush with annoyance.

"I have not the slightest intention of doing so. I just thought it odd that nobody has informed on the thieves."

"I didn't mean to suggest that you wanted the money, Martin. I was going to say that it would be very unwise for anyone to risk such a thing. These men are serious, the raid was meticulously planned and ruthlessly executed. They almost killed a man who just happened to walk past."

Day prompted him to go on. Andreas paused as if considering whether to share the details, then clearly thought it would do no harm.

"The property in question was a large, isolated house in the hills some distance from Sparta. Security was adequate, but the employee in charge of it was working with the gang. They got away with practically the whole collection of antiquities, which the owner kept on display rather than locked away. The collector had been drugged so he came to no harm, but the unexpected happened. A local man decided to take some food to a neighbour, walked along the road past the big house and saw the robbery taking place. The criminals saw him. He was badly beaten."

"Was he alright?" asked Helen.

"Eventually. He recovered after a long stay in hospital."

"Were any of the items ever found, or the thieves caught?"

"Nothing was recovered at the time and very little since," said Andreas. "The owner had a detailed catalogue of his collection, so the antiquities squad have kept a close eye on the illegal market. One or two things have turned up, but very few. We think that, unusually, the haul was divided between three key men who had the job of arranging the sales. They've either sold the goods on successfully or, more likely, are holding on to them until it's safe to get rid of them.

"We're pretty sure we know who those three men are. They all have history with the police. However, knowing who the criminals are and having enough evidence to arrest them all are two quite different things. And we want them all, not just the small people. This robbery, which we call the Taygetus Raid, was carried out by seven men, one of whom came from Naxos. I believe he is one of the three who took a share of the haul. So you can understand why I'm here. Without new evidence there's nothing we can do, but with the discovery of the bronze horse figure I think we may have a chance. It's possible that more items from the same robbery are hidden somewhere on Naxos. I need to find them." He stared straight at Day. "This must remain strictly between the three of us, Martin. I know I can trust you."

"Of course," said Day, aware that Andreas was thinking of one or two occasions in the recent past when he had acted independently. The thought also occurred that Andreas might, in a round-about way, be asking for his help. 'I know I can trust you.' What did that really mean?

"Can I ask the name of this man, the one you're looking for on Naxos? Or is he to have a code name like the robbery?"

Andreas looked unsure whether to be annoyed or amused. To Day's surprise he decided to answer.

"The name is Artsanos," he said. "Sotiris Artsanos."

"Artsanos? You know his brother has a bar in Halki?"

"Martin, try to stay out of this and leave it to the police. Of course I know about the brother, I have some experience of police work. I gather you know him? Be very careful, you must do nothing and say nothing to anyone of what I've told you."

That was clear enough, even for Day.

16

That afternoon Day sat once again on the balcony of his house staring vacantly at the valley and not seeing it. Helen had taken the car to the Bazeos Tower where she was hosting some discussion groups. Day was therefore grounded. He would ask Ben if he'd like to come over, but first he wanted to do some thinking.

Andreas had given him the name of Sotiris Artsanos. Surely Andreas intended him to do something with this piece of information, which otherwise the policeman would surely have kept to himself. There were some things only a civilian could do, Day thought, whereas the police had to follow procedures. Besides, to understand Ricky's death he had to check everything to do with the increasingly intriguing Di Quercia Tower, a place connected with Sotiris Artsanos's family past.

He considered what he knew of the present-day family. There was Kostas, owner of The Black Acorn and about Day's age, roughly forty. Sotiris was meant to be the older of the brothers, and the sister, Evangelia, a little younger. That accounted for the siblings, and Athina had said the elder family members were probably gone. He must not forget Adonis, the ageless and handsome Adonis, Evangelia's husband

and a member of the family by marriage. He pondered what the wife of Adonis might be like: Evangelia must be a beautiful woman, he thought, or a very confident one, to marry such a man.

What did he know of Sotiris, the suspected member of the Taygettus Raid gang? He had grown up in or near the abandoned village of Sifones. He was rumoured to have become a sheep farmer, which could simply be a cover for his other activities. Aristos had said that Sotiris may have left the island; for the long term, or to meet his buyers?

"So," Day said aloud, despite there being nobody to hear. "Assuming Sotiris is one of the men who carried out the Taygetus Raid, did he hide the antiquities in the cellar of the tower? Did he later move them elsewhere, carelessly leaving behind the tiny horse? Surely not, surely he would have taken everything. Leaving that aside, if he had decided to move the stolen goods, where would he have taken them?"

Day had a rather good idea about that. Where better than a deserted village, especially one which the thief already knew well?

Day steepled his fingers, beginning to enjoy himself. He would go and explore the abandoned village of Sifones. He would tell Andreas: there was no reason not to work with Andreas on this. If the stolen antiquities could be found, it would give Andreas enough evidence to arrest Sotiris Artsanos.

He got up and poured himself a glass of cold water from the bottle in the fridge. It was probably just a way of putting off the next thing he needed to think about. Ricky.

When it came to Ricky, he didn't know where to start. He refused to believe that the discovery of the bronze horse and Ricky's death in the same location and in the same week were unconnected, but he could not imagine what the connection was.

Ben had not taken Ricky to the tower. Day believed Ben, rightly or wrongly, and he would stick with that. Ricky had told Ben that morning not to collect him. This seemed to rule out something happening that Ricky could not have foreseen, such as Ricky being forced to go to the tower against his will. Ricky's lies, as Day concluded they were, meant that Ricky had gone to the tower willingly, and had already decided to do so before leaving home that morning.

Day allowed his imagination to follow Ricky to the tower. He had climbed the scaffolding up to the parapet and had probably been pushed from the top. It made no sense. Who hated him enough to do that on Naxos? Could he have committed suicide? No, the witness, the car, the other man. And why go to the Di Quercia Tower at all?

With a sigh, Day picked up his mobile and called Ben.

Day watched from the door as a small hire car parked in the road outside. It was almost a match for Day's own Fiat, which had once been a hire car itself. Ben got out and gave a small wave. He looked tired and his face seemed to have lost something of its roundness.

"So this is where you live?" he said, looking round the main room. "It's very quiet, isn't it?"

"Well, it certainly isn't Brighton. Come through, we can talk on the balcony."

He made coffee and Ben began to relax. Day asked how he had been treated by the police.

"They were very fair, really. I had a couple of visits from an English-speaking lawyer, which was really helpful. I think I have you to thank for that, don't I?"

"Least I could do," Day said. "Tell me what happened."

Ben took a drink of his coffee and dragged his eyes off the view across the valley.

"Every time they interviewed me they asked about my relationship with Ricky. I could tell they wanted me to reveal that we had relationship problems and admit to killing him, but I just kept telling them the truth. I think the inspector soon realised he was on the wrong track, but it was all a bit relentless. I thought it would never end.

"Then a different policeman took over from him, someone more senior, a big fair-haired man with fierce blue eyes who gave me the third degree. It didn't change the facts. The lawyer just kept telling me not to give up. They had to let me go in the end."

Ben pinched his nose with the thumb and middle finger of his spare hand as if forestalling tears, then put his coffee cup carefully down on the table.

"What I don't understand, Martin, is why Ricky said I was going to pick him up when he'd told me not to. Was Ricky lying to me? Or are the other people lying? What do you think?"

Day said he didn't know.

"It makes me absolutely desperate that I might never know the truth! You wouldn't think it could get any worse, but it really matters that he might have lied to me."

Ben stopped abruptly to gain control of himself. Day waited.

"I'm afraid I didn't really know him after all…"

He stared resolutely over the railings towards the opposite hillside, hanging onto his composure. After a minute Day offered more coffee. The business of pouring it covered the time until Ben could continue.

"Ricky wasn't … he wasn't someone who talked much about himself. He didn't tell me about his life before we got together, not in detail. I respected that, it had nothing to do with our relationship, and I didn't need to know. It was obvious that he'd had more experience of life than I had. Sometimes I thought he wanted to forget the past. He was the kind of person who lived in the moment. He could be impulsive, spontaneous, and he didn't miss an opportunity to do anything exciting and new. That suited me. That's how we ended up coming to Naxos. One moment he was reading about the Festival, the next he'd booked our flights. For Ricky, time wasn't to be wasted."

"Carpe diem. You say it suited you? Did you want to come here?"

"I didn't mind, and once we got here I quite enjoyed it all. Now, I wish we'd never come."

He gave a weak smile and seemed to check Day's face for a reaction. It was unfortunately time for Day to broach the subject he least wanted to discuss.

"I have to ask a difficult question. Was Ricky also impulsive when it came to … personal relationships?"

Not only did Ben immediately understand; Day thought that he had wanted to be asked.

"Sometimes," Ben nodded.

"Often?"

"No, not often, and it was never a major thing. It only happened twice, in fact, and both were before we were married. I know what you're thinking, Martin. Yes, I did wonder whether Ricky might have been meeting someone that afternoon, but only because I can't understand otherwise why he lied to me. We were OK together, more than OK, I give you my word…"

"Let's keep it between ourselves, then. The police might think it gives you a motive for killing Ricky, which is the last thing you need. Leave it with me for a while. I intend to get to the truth or die in the attempt, as they say."

"Okay. Though I don't see how you're going to do that. And I hope you're joking about dying in the attempt!"

"Have you been given permission to take Ricky home yet?"

"No, the coroner still hasn't released the body. The embassy were reluctant to get involved while I was under suspicion, but yesterday they told me that there would be a cremation locally and the ashes would be signed over to me. I can't get my head round the need for cremation! Still, after that I can go home. It's not so easy arranging to take somebody's ashes on a plane, but the solicitor has been helpful on that."

"All very awful," muttered Day. Ben appeared not to hear.

"Then I'll have to arrange some kind of funeral at home, because Ricky has a sister and a step-mother who will want to have a ceremony. Oh, I don't know, it's all a nightmare! Once this is all over I think I'll leave Brighton. We were renting our place, so I won't renew the lease. I need to start somewhere new. There'll be work for me in London."

"Don't be too hasty on that. All your contacts must be in Brighton. Better to find a new flat, maybe, but stay where you have friends."

"You might be right. I'll think about it."

When Ben had gone, Day realised it was mid-afternoon and he still hadn't had anything to eat. He had no appetite, his mind was racing and not only from the coffee. He opened his computer and sat for a few moments working out the best way to approach the problem. He was not interested in Ben's suspicions of a promiscuous liaison between Ricky and some stranger on the day of his death, which surely the police would be considering anyway, although it should not be completely dismissed. Something far more interesting was engaging Day's imagination. He had woken in the night and found himself thinking about it.

He was sure it was important that Ricky's name had rung a bell in the wise head of the esteemed Curator. Aristos was never fanciful, and Day had never known his memory to let him down. If Aristos felt he had heard Ricky's name before, and in connection with Naxos, Day believed him. A new link between Ricky and this island might prove very illuminating and divert the attention of the police away from Ben.

He decided to start with an online search of the past issues of the local paper, The Naxian. It turned out to be no simple matter. He got access easily enough, but it seemed he needed special permission to open any issue that was over two years old. Every so often his enquiry would be frozen and he would be required to go through the permission process again. It was tedious, but for Day it was not unusual: sometimes he did this kind of research for weeks on end. Not, admittedly, in a modern context, and not usually in connection with a murder, but Day could be a plodder if the situation demanded, and he was still working in exactly the same position when Helen returned at four thirty.

The bad news was that he had found no mention of Ricky Somerset on Naxos at all, and had already searched back over twelve years.

Helen went off to her room saying she would see him on the balcony at seven, and Day decided to take a break and enjoy that most Greek of habits, a restorative late afternoon siesta.

17

The next day was Saturday 20th October, the last day of the Naxos Literary Festival and the day when Helen was due to give the keynote lecture during the afternoon.

For many of the Festival guests this was their last night on Naxos, including most of those staying at the Elias House. Ben was the exception, but this would be Day's only chance to meet the others and ask his questions.

There was no need to set off for the Bazeos Tower until late morning. Helen thought that the ideal way to prepare for her lecture was a trip out for coffee, and Day suggested somewhere with a view of the sea.

"We could go to Vasilios's place, but let's drive to Agia Anna instead. We can sit at one of the cafés right at the edge of the water."

The drive from Filoti to Agia Anna took half an hour and gave them the chance to top up the car with petrol on the way. As they passed through Halki, Day's thoughts returned to The Black Acorn bar and its genial owner, Kostas.

"Do you remember Andreas told us about a Naxos man the police have connected to the robbery in the Taygetus?"

"Yes, Sotiris somebody."

"Sotiris Artsanos, brother of Kostas who owns The Black Acorn. I wonder how much he might know about his brother's criminal career."

"Oh! You're seriously getting involved with all this, aren't you, Martin? Despite what Andreas said."

"Of course I am! I was in at the start when the bronze horse was found, we were at the fire, and above all I'm close to Ben. I thought you'd understood."

He was unable to moderate the exasperation in his tone. Really, she should know that he had to see this through now. He felt her hand on his arm.

"Sorry," she said. "Of course I understand. When we get to Agia Anna you can tell me your ideas and maybe I can help."

Day had no need to wait, and immediately shared his thoughts with her concerning the elusive Sotiris and his sheep farm, the probable cache of stolen antiquities somewhere on the island, and the abandoned village of Sifones which might offer a wealth of suitable hiding places.

"Before you say anything," he added, "I'm going to talk to Andreas before I make any moves this time."

"Very sensible. Unusually so!"

"However, he thinks that Ricky's death must be connected to the art thieves. I really can't agree with him there. Ricky Somerset wasn't the type to be involved with big-time criminals."

Helen suppressed a sigh and flexed her fingers against the dashboard.

"Right. What do you want me to do?" she said as they reached the car park at Agia Anna.

"Just listen to me and tell me what you think."

They were soon sitting with coffee at a beach taverna at Agia Anna. The sun was quite high in the sky behind the taverna, sending sparkling shivers over the sea. They could hear voices from the kitchen, deliveries arriving, and a girl sweeping the sand from the terrace. There was something perfect about having the place to themselves, their feet on the sand, their table only a few feet from the edge of the sea.

"I've decided what I'm going to do next," said Day without preamble. "Your talk this afternoon, or rather the reception afterwards, will give us an opportunity to chat to some interesting people. Athina told me that Maria Di Quercia will be there. She owns the tower and commissioned Nick's restoration. I want to hear what she says. The two other writers who have been staying at the Elias House will be there too. I haven't had a chance to speak to them yet, and I want to hear what Ricky may have told them about his plans on the day he died. And the man in charge of the catering, Adonis, is apparently married to Sotiris's sister …"

"My God, Martin, it's all very incestuous, isn't it? It feels like everyone's related to everyone else. And I feel really sorry for poor Maria - I've talked to her quite a bit recently. She was very upset when she heard about Ricky, especially because he died at her tower."

Day suddenly remembered why they were sitting on the beach at Agia Anna - to pass an hour or two quietly before Helen gave her lecture. He was briefly struck with a slight guilt.

"I'm really looking forward to your talk. Have you invited people like Aristos and Nick?"

"Athina has invited local celebrities, so that of course includes our friend Aristos, famed throughout Naxos. Nick has been invited too, and I've invited Andreas."

"Ah, good," said Day. He focussed on a fishing boat that was slowly moving from right to left just off shore. He had a few reservations about the last name; he hoped Andreas wouldn't cramp his style.

"Are you all ready? What's your lecture about?"

"The Committee asked me to speak about my own writing and refer to my own books, which is what people tend to want. I'm going to make the subject more general, though. The talk is called 'The Role of Error in Fiction'."

Day laughed. "Nice! Everyone can relate to making errors, and if you make a mistake this afternoon you can pretend it was deliberate!"

"Idiot! In a nutshell, I'm going to say that the idea of error is pivotal in my fiction both thematically and in terms of the plot, and invite people to consider the wider implications of … are you still listening, Martin?"

"Of course! It's a brilliant subject. And I think Andreas would say that it's as central to crime investigation as to fiction. In fact, you've just given me an idea. How like you! I wonder how human error might have played some part in all this."

"'To err is human'," she murmured with a smile, largely ignoring him, and buried her toes in the warm sand.

The mid-afternoon sun had turned the old stone walls of the Bazeos Tower from grey to pale amber. There was a sense that the people who were gathered in front of the facade to enjoy the atmosphere before the last event of the Festival shared a nostalgia for the friendships they had made in the last few weeks. There were people here who would continue to talk to each other across the continents for some time to come. English was the prevalent language of the Festival, but the writers had come from Greece, the USA, the UK, Italy, Germany and France.

Day stood with Nick and Deppi watching the people around them. Helen was inside making final preparations. Aristos and his wife Rania stood talking with the owner of the Bazeos Tower. Athina walked towards him, her narrow red skirt apparently not impeding her progress.

"Martin, lovely to see you! Nick, hello again." She kissed Day warmly on both cheeks and, in a more nonchalant manner, did the same to Nick. Nick grinned and introduced his wife.

"Athina, this is my wife Despina. Deppi, this is Athina, who's in charge of running the Festival."

Day looked on, very aware of his different relationships with the two women. He watched them laughing at a joke which Day had missed. He caught Deppi looking at him, then Athina wound her arm through his and pulled him slightly to one side, whispering in his ear.

"I'm going to bring you a present, *agapi mou*: the little wife of Adonis, Evangelia. You can meet another oak sapling and tell me what you think when you come to dinner. She's been working this morning and now she's waiting for Adonis to take her home. I shall tell her that you've met her brother Kostas, then you will have something to talk about. I don't think she knows anyone else here."

Before Day could say anything, Athina had sailed off into the crowd and returned with a pretty girl of about thirty who looked shy and embarrassed. Athina quickly vanished again. Evangelia wore a white blouse and dark trousers, and her hair was plaited and twisted round her head. Day felt the girl's nervousness like a pinch in the arm.

"Hello, I'm Martin. These are my friends, Deppi and Nick. You're Kostas's sister? What a lovely bar he has there in Halki. He made us very welcome the other day."

The girl became more confident as she spoke of her brother and sister-in-law, and how hard they had worked to build The Black Acorn into a good business. She also told them that she lived in Apeiranthos with her husband, and that she worked as a waitress in the summer. Day began to adjust his initial impression of Evangelia. At first she had been socially uneasy, but now it was clear that she was, in fact, a strong personality with plenty to say. She asked Day about himself, and then chatted with Nick and Deppi until their easy conversation was brought to an end by the arrival of her husband.

The good-looking Adonis smoothly excused himself and his wife, saying that he was going to take Evangelia home before returning to work again during the post-event reception. Hands were shaken, and Evangelia and Adonis walked away towards the car park.

"Wow!" said Nick under his breath. It was not necessary to explain his remark, as the beauty of the Greek couple was evident to them all. "Helen of Troy still lives and breathes, and also Paris."

"Hector called Paris 'fair to see but with neither wit nor courage'," said Day almost under his breath. The quote from Homer had come unsought into his mind, but he wondered whether he should give it more thought when he had the time.

"You seemed to know the girl, Martin," said Deppi. "What's the story?"

"I've never met her before, but I've met one of her brothers. It seems their family is distantly related to the owners of the Di Quercia Tower."

"Look, I know this is a bit odd," said Nick, "but I've met that woman before. She arrived at the Di Quercia Tower one day while I was there on my own. I wasn't sure it was her just now, she looks different today and she didn't seem to recognise me. It was definitely the same woman, though, I'm sure."

"When was this, Nick?"

"Let's see - Orestis and I had been there with the scaffolding people. They'd finished and everyone but me had left, and I was finishing up taking some photos. So it was before the fire, but after we found the horse. Evangelia just turned up on foot saying she often walked that way."

"Do you remember anything else she said?"

"She was curious about what we were doing and about the restoration. She'd known the building since her childhood. She said she felt a bit sad that the old place was going to be changed. It's something people often say, they get sentimental about ruins."

"Did she want to go inside?"

"Yes, she was a nice woman so I showed her round a bit, just on the ground floor so she could look up at the scaffolding on the inside. She seemed very interested."

Deppi gave a small laugh, putting her hand round Nick's waist to reassure him that she was teasing. "Well, she clearly made quite an impression on you, Nick, I'm surprised you didn't recognise her straight away today! They're a good-looking couple. Funny, though, until I realised Evangelia was his wife I'd assumed Adonis was gay."

At that moment a hand bell was rung ceremoniously from the parapet of the Bazeos Tower to signify that the final event would soon begin and guests were invited into the building. As they began to move inside, Day's eyes could rest on Deppi unobserved, allowing him to enjoy the fall of her long dark hair over her black dress and suntanned shoulders.

A cat can look at a queen, he told himself, not for the first time.

18

Kyrie Tsirmpas, the Chairman of the Naxos Literary Festival Committee, a title he clearly relished, ascended to the small platform after Helen's lecture. He was a small, round man with the stoicism to wear a suit and tie on a warm afternoon in a crowded room. He proposed a vote of thanks to the speaker and, after the resulting applause, formally closed the Festival. It had been, he said, an exceptional series of events, and he thanked everyone for their participation and enthusiasm.

"It's a very great sadness to all of us," he concluded, his tone becoming serious, "that a tragedy has occurred which has cast a terrible shadow over the Festival this year and struck each of us to the very core. We remember Ricky Somerset with the greatest respect, admiration and warmth, and we shall keep a special place in our hearts for him here on Naxos. Our thoughts are with his family and close friends.

"I'm certain that Ricky would not want us to curtail our evening on his account, however. I invite everyone to the final reception of the Festival, in the courtyard in front of the facade, where we may enjoy a glass of wine with the new friends we have made this year. Can I ask you to join me in thanking the owner of this wonderful venue,

Kyrie Bazeos, for hosting the Festival, and once again Mrs Helen Aitchison, our Writer in Residence."

Out of the silence that followed the reminder of Ricky's death came generous applause. It was hard to tell whether it was for Helen and *Kyrie* Bazeos, or because the Chairman's speech had come to an end. Chairs were scraped noisily in the vaulted stone room and everyone began to talk at once.

As most people drifted towards the exit, Day fought his way through them towards the platform and Helen. Several people made way for him in the face of his momentum.

"No mistake there, Helen," he said, releasing her from a hug. "That was outstanding! Congratulations! Come and have a glass of wine with me outside, I want to show off that I know you!"

They made their way to the front courtyard where Adonis and his staff were serving drinks from a long table beside an old vine-covered wall. Day fetched wine for Helen and himself, and returned to find her standing with a woman who could only be, in his opinion, Maria Di Quercia. She had an air of poise and distinction, and was dressed with artistic taste and no shortage of money. Her voice travelled across the space between them with elan. Day had never required that word before, but it came to him now without hesitation. Elan, panache, flair - in whatever language you preferred, these were the words to describe Signora Maria Di Quercia.

Helen looked up at Day's approach and accepted the glass of wine. Day gave the other to Maria Di Quercia with a small bow.

"Martin, this is Maria. Maria, my friend Martin Day. He was hoping to meet you."

"How wonderful to meet *you*," said Maria. "Helen has told me that you're a historian. I expect you feel at home in this exceptional building?"

Day found it hard to guess her age, and it absolutely did not matter that she was no longer a young woman.

"It's stunning, and so beautifully restored. I know you intended to restore your own tower. I hope the work can still go ahead?"

"Oh, what a very, very sad and tragic thing to happen. The poor man. His memory will always be in the stones of my unfortunate tower. Eventually, yes, we will be able to complete the work. It will be a family home once again, and I'm thinking that when we're not living in it, it could be used in some way for people's benefit, like they do here, as an art space, or for teaching young people about the past."

"A very good idea," said Day. "How long has the tower been in your family?"

"Six generations that we know about so far, and it must be considerably longer than that. The family left Naxos a very long time ago. I want to do some genealogical research myself, and really understand our history."

"Did you know that you have distant relatives still living on Naxos?"

Maria had not known, and pressed Day for details. He suddenly felt on difficult ground and wished he had thought before speaking. It was entirely possible that one of her relatives was not somebody to be proud of.

"I'll send some details to you through Helen. I suppose you're going back to Italy now that the Festival has finished?"

"I'll be leaving in a week or so. I still have some arrangements to make with the restoration company. Thank you, I'll look forward to hearing from you. Let's definitely keep in touch, Helen. Thank you for an inspiring talk. Goodnight!"

Maria Di Quercia bestowed a graceful smile on them and moved towards the group which had formed round the Curator and *Kyrie* Bazeos. Day saw Aristos glance over her shoulder and wink at him. The wink said that Aristos knew he was not going to be able to get away.

Day took Helen's empty glass and returned to the serving table. By the time he got back to her, Andreas was there. Day decided not to impose himself on them, passed a glass of wine to Helen and went in search of Athina.

He eventually found her.

"Athina, I'd really like to meet Mrs Savage and David Worthington, the people staying in my house. Do you think you could introduce us, please?"

Athina scanned the gathering.

"Ah, there's David's wife … yes, they're all standing together. Let's go and join them."

She led Day adeptly through the crowd.

"May we join you? This is Martin, your host at the accommodation. I thought you'd like to meet him before you go home."

They chatted for a while about the house and the island, the Festival and the Bazeos Tower, until it was impossible to avoid the elephant in the room, Ricky's death.

"I'm so relieved that the police have released poor Ben," said Mrs Savage. "Clearly a big mistake to arrest him in the first place. A nicer young man you couldn't hope to meet. Poor Ben - and poor Ricky, of course."

"You can see why the police suspected Ben, of course," David Worthington pointed out. "Once a few people had told them that Ricky was expecting to be collected by Ben that afternoon, suspicion was bound to fall on him."

"Did you hear Ricky say that yourself? In so many words?" asked Day.

"Oh yes, lots of us did. He wanted to tell us they'd be having lobster at the local taverna, the one we like across the bay, Vasilios's place."

"He sounded so happy about it," agreed Melanie Savage. "It was to be a romantic dinner for their wedding anniversary, I think he said."

Day nodded; this was the first he had heard of a wedding anniversary. It seemed Ricky had been an imaginative liar.

He realised that David was asking him something, and had to ask him to repeat it.

"I said, do you want more wine? I'm going over to get mine refilled, would you like a top-up?"

"I'll come with you," said Day. They reached the serving table and David ensured his own glass was nicely full before they began their way back to the group. Athina had moved on and Melanie Savage and David's wife were deep in conversation.

"That man, the one in charge of the drinks," David muttered, "Ricky couldn't drag himself away from him. I guess a man with those looks would be hard to ignore if you were of Ricky's persuasion. It was just too blatant, everyone knew what was going on!"

Day recoiled. The unmissable note of homophobia surprised and repelled him. He handed a glass of wine to Melanie Savage, nodded politely to everyone and rejoined Helen and Andreas.

"Martin has been off doing his investigations again, Andrea," Helen teased as soon as Day came within earshot. "I can't control him."

"I was just chatting to the people who have been staying at the Elias House. Nothing exciting, I assure you."

Andreas eyed him curiously. "I'm guessing you think we shouldn't be looking at Sotiris Artsanos for killing Ricky Somerset?" he said somewhat sharply.

"I *feel* there's more to it, though I don't know what. Feelings are not acceptable as evidence."

"Indeed not. I have to disagree with you about this. There are two ways in which the robbery and the murder could be linked, Martin, and I'm sure one will turn out to be the truth. Either Ricky Somerset was working with Artsanos, they argued, and Artsanos killed him. Or Ricky had discovered what Artsanos was up to and either blackmailed him or threatened to go to the police. Again, Artsanos killed him."

"Neither seem very likely to me, Andrea. It would have been out of character for Ricky."

"Well, so be it, give me something else. It's unlike you not to come up with a creative solution."

19

Day's enthusiasm for searching the deserted village with Andreas diminished that evening. He made a new plan, one about which he felt excited as soon as he had decided on it.

Day liked the mountain village of Apeiranthos. It was a uniquely charming place, and there was a café he was particularly fond of, although he would not have time to linger there today. He had formed a fresh conjecture concerning one of Apeiranthos's residents, and he planned to call on them uninvited.

The drive would take only fifteen minutes following the road from Filoti past the Di Quercia Tower. He was in no rush. At the tower he drove a short way down the track to check on it, and found the police cordon had been removed and some men were discussing the structure, possibly some of Nick's team. He reversed back to the main road and drove on to Apeiranthos.

On the slopes of Mount Fanari, the second highest peak of Naxos, the white buildings of Apeiranthos shone above the spreading valley. There was no view of the sea from Apeiranthos, so you could almost forget you were on an island. At about six hundred feet above sea level, the azure sky felt nearer than the Aegean, and the village's command over the landscape was as inspiring as any vista of the sea.

He parked the Fiat at the top of a hill just outside the village, and strolled down towards the square. The village council restricted the number of vehicles allowed to enter the streets, and the residential roads were as peaceful as usual. The village was always a joy to wander through, bright and well kept. The houses were made of white-painted stone and pale marble, and in places the influence of the Venetians was still apparent. Coats of arms dating from that era appeared over some doorways, and near the centre of the village was another of Naxos's Venetian towers, this one restored and imposing.

The owner of Day's favourite café gave him a wave as he passed. He regretted not having the time to spend a pleasant half hour there in the mild sunshine, watching the passers-by. Listening to the locals from one of the pavement tables was particularly enjoyable in Apeiranthos, where you could still hear a dialect based on Cretan. Day liked to overhear conversations in the café and try to understand this local language. As far as the Greek language was concerned, he would never stop learning. His Greek could be described as a fluent and polite hotchpotch of the Ancient Greek he had learned at school and university, modern formal Greek called *katharevousa* which he had learned at a class in Athens, and true modern Greek, the language of everyday speech, called *demotiki*. Every so often a local would chuckle at Day's Greek, but in general they liked him for it.

Athina had told him how to find the house he wanted. She knew every inch of Apeiranthos from her years guiding tourist groups, and her directions had been clear. The narrow lane rose in wide steps that had been moulded by the footfalls of generations, and passed beneath stone balconies where opposing houses almost touched. Athina had told him to look out for a bright yellow ELTA post box attached to one wall, and there it was. Evangelia and Adonis's house had ornate, grey-painted railings edging the steps to their front door, and the white marble doorstep was scrubbed clean. The house was traditional, very small, part of the fabric of the old street, and he guessed it was hardly larger than his one-bedroom apartment in Athens.

He was taking a risk calling on Evangelia when her husband was at work, but he needed to talk to her alone, and wanted to take her by surprise. He hesitated at the door.

His knock sounded very loud in the quiet street. He heard a lock being turned inside and Evangelia opened the door, her hair dishevelled, a different woman to the self-possessed girl he had met at the Bazeos Tower. She clearly recognised him. Her face expressed relief rather than alarm, so Day adopted his most courteous smile and within minutes was invited in. The tradition of Greek hospitality to strangers, the so-called *filoxenia* for which Greek people are justly famous, had opened another door to him.

The door led directly from the street into a small living room which was neat and clean, almost as if he had been expected. Day registered white walls, a tiled floor, old wooden furniture and a small window graced by a lace curtain, all elements he had expected to see. On the walls were family photographs in black and white or sepia, showing the generations of the family: individual pictures of a mother and father, photographs showing a grandmother with a small child in a white dress, a fisherman by his boat, an old wedding picture, and a small class of school children. Copper pots decorated every surface, and a carved and painted wooden chest that looked very old stood in the far corner. The table, the sofa and every possible surface was covered with the locally woven cloth for which the island was known. Day noticed a shotgun propped against the wall, and quickly looked away from it.

"Please, sit down," she said. "Would you like something to drink? A coffee?"

"That's very kind but no, thank you," he said in his best Greek, accepting her invitation to sit on the settee. "I apologise for calling on you without warning, but I'm hoping we can talk about something very important."

"I have no idea how I can help you."

Day was inclined to believe her. That suited him well.

"Your husband is at work, I expect?" he asked casually. "I trust he's well?"

"Oh yes, thank you."

Day nodded, then looked at the young woman directly. "A friend has told me that he met a young lady recently at the old Di Quercia Tower, just a day or two before the terrible fire. That was you, I think?"

The woman's face hardened. Day even thought that her face had lost some of its colour, but in the filtered light from the curtained window it was impossible to tell. She said nothing, and he was forced to go on.

"He's quite sure it was you, actually. At the Bazeos Tower last night he recognised you. Can you remember your conversation with him?"

"Yes, now I remember. He spoke Greek with an Australian accent. He told me about the work they were going to do on the old ruin. Why is that important?"

"It's a very long way from here to the Di Quercia Tower, and Apeiranthos has many more attractive and easier walks that you could have chosen."

"That's true, but I have walked them many times and I wanted to go further that day."

Day adopted a reassuring manner.

"I think you had a very particular reason for going to the tower. I'd like to help you, believe me. In fact, it's extremely important that you let me help you. The man you're afraid of is unpredictable and violent, as you know very well."

She shook her head as if to make him go away.

"Remember, if I've worked out why you went to the tower that day, *he* may soon do the same."

The young woman, who had sat on the edge of one of the dining chairs, laid her hand on the tablecloth as if to steady herself and looked at him with wide eyes and an open mouth.

"I know about the little horse statue," said Day quietly.

"How do you know about that?" Her voice was small and choked.

"The restorers found it in the cellar and took it to the museum, where I was shown it. I think you knew it was in the tower and went to get it that afternoon."

"I went to get it back when I heard about the building work starting. I knew that if the builders discovered it, everyone would find out…"

"You mean that you wanted to avoid people finding out that your brother, Sotiris, was involved in the robbery in the Peloponnese where it was stolen?"

The woman shook her head and tightened her lips. Her fingers were playing with the tassels at the edge of the tablecloth as if the action brought her some comfort.

"As I said before," Day said quietly, "I won't be the only one to work this out, and your brother will come and find you to ask where the horse is now. Do you know how valuable that little statue is? It's more than two thousand years old, and people will pay many thousands of dollars for it. And when your brother discovers that it's gone, he's going to be very angry. He'll want it back, and you won't be able to give it to him. It wasn't very clever to steal from a thief as violent as your brother."

Evangelia's eyes darted to the corner of the room where her husband's shotgun stood propped against the wall. Many men in rural Greece kept a shotgun for ridding themselves of vermin, or shooting rabbits and birds for the pot. This one, however, was not safely locked away. For the first time Day realised his vulnerability here alone.

"It was a beautiful little thing," Evangelia said wistfully.

Day's heart began to slow to a more normal rate. Now he simply wanted to get this done with.

"Evangelia, you're not responsible for your brother, but you can't deny that you know what kind of man he is. You can either sit here waiting for him to burst in like an angry bull, or you can put a stop to it all. Then you can be safe. Why protect him?"

"If he was your brother, if you lived here, if you'd spent the last fifteen years trying to live a decent life, maybe you wouldn't need to ask me! Sotiris has always been a bully. My other brother argued with Sotiris and got free of him, but I can't. Sotiris won't let me. If people find out about him, I'll have to leave. And I have nowhere to go!"

Day realised that he had broken through her defences. It was now just a matter of time. He checked his watch.

"Tell me how you knew that the bronze horse was hidden in the Di Quercia Tower."

She looked almost relieved to talk.

"The people that own the tower were once part of our family, and my father always said the tower was rightfully ours. My brothers and I used to play in it when we were young. I knew every inch of the old place. We all did. I've known for years that Sotiris hides things there while he finds a buyer. I used to go and run my hands over the beautiful objects. I fell in love with the little horse as soon as I saw it, and one day I just took it home with me on impulse. The next day, before I could return it, Sotiris moved all his bags to a new hiding place and didn't notice the horse was gone. I put the horse back in the hiding place so that he'd think it had fallen out."

Day watched her quietly. He was certain now that she would tell him everything he needed to hear.

"I heard in the village that the Di Quercia Tower was to be restored," she said. "I went to the tower that day to get the little horse because I thought the builders would find it and it would all come out about Sotiris. The Australian showed me round but I couldn't get to the cellar."

"By that time the horse was already in the safe at the Naxos Museum."

"Ah. Well, what happens now? Sotiris will miss the horse, he knows everything of value that he steals, he's finding a buyer for everything…"

"He'll probably find out that the builders took the horse, and hopefully think he dropped it himself, as you planned. But you need him out of your life, and I can help. Do you know his other hiding places?"

She nodded. "In Sifones somewhere, and maybe in Panagia Chrysopigi."

"An old church? Where is it?"

"It's between here and the village of Danakos."

"Okay. Sotiris is away at the moment, right? You must go to the police before he returns. Tell them everything, don't keep anything from them, and they'll take care of you. Go right away, this afternoon."

"I can't. Adonis is home this afternoon. He's due any time for lunch."

"Then tomorrow morning, but make sure you go."

"They won't believe me."

"I'll speak to them for you. They will believe you, and they'll help you."

"Why are you doing this for me?"

"It's a long story. You're expecting Adonis?"

"Yes. He won't be happy that I'm talking to you alone like this."

Day glanced at the shotgun in the corner and was inclined to agree with her.

"I'm going. Don't change your mind. Go to the police as soon as you can."

He got up and Evangelia opened the front door. Adonis was at the far end of the street, locking his car. His perfectly shaped head, delineated by sleek black hair, was looking down and he hadn't seen Day yet. The door closed quickly behind Day and he slipped away, taking a detour before re-joining the street. He passed Adonis on a flight of steps a little way from the house. Adonis looked up and his face registered recognition, surprise, suspicion.

Only when he had reached the square and started to walk uphill to his car did Day relax. He must speak to Andreas next, but it would be necessary to choose his words very carefully. Andreas was rather against Day's tendency to take matters into his own hands.

20

Day could not stop thinking about Evangelia as he drove home. He had achieved what he had set out to do, so why did he feel he was missing something important?

The three Artsanos siblings had chosen different lives. Kostas had devoted himself to hard work and a settled marriage, and had broken off all ties with his dishonest brother. Evangelia had married an attractive man and set up home in a respectable village. Sotiris had become a thief, a violent man, and kept his sister under his control.

Was it all a bit too neat, though? Were the life-stories he had invented for the family too stereotypical? He was reassured that the facts did seem to bear him out. The police already knew that Sotiris belonged to the gang who had committed the Taygetus Raid. Athina had vouched for Kostas's character, as had Aristos. That left Evangelia, whose behaviour had seemed genuine enough. If she kept her word and reported her brother to the police, Day would be reassured.

Before he realised it, he had arrived at Filoti and parked outside his house. Inside he found Helen talking on her phone, clearly pleased about something.

"Hi, Martin" she said, closing the call. "That was the Chairman, thanking me again. People are so polite in Greece! Where did you get to this morning?"

She asked in a tone that suggested he might reply that he had been swimming, meeting a friend or, more likely, stocking up with new wine. Day threw himself into a chair.

"I went to Apeiranthos and talked to that girl we met last night, the one married to the catering manager at the Festival."

Helen's blank expression reminded him that she had not been with him when Evangelia had been introduced. He told her about the young wife of Adonis.

"Evangelia admitted to leaving the bronze horse in the Di Quercia Tower, having removed it from her brother Sotiris's cache of stolen antiquities because she liked it. I've told her to go to the police tomorrow."

"Oh Martin, you're doing it again! That was something you could have left to the police, you know."

"To Andreas, you mean?" Day snapped. "I see. Well, don't worry, I'm sure he'll get the credit."

He realised they were about to have an argument. Crossly he announced his intention to work in his room, picked up his laptop and closed the door behind him rather firmly. He put the computer on his table and didn't look at it again for several hours.

Instead, he lay on the bed with his arms crossed. He carefully thought though every detail of what he knew about the tower, the murder and the robbery, and one or two new ideas occurred to him. Then he reflected on what Helen had said. The more he thought about it, the more convinced he became that he was in the wrong. He splashed water on his face in the bathroom, found he had no clean shirts, and, in an even worse mood, put on an old jumper and went to apologise to Helen.

She had anticipated this and gave him no opportunity to provoke another disagreement.

"Just pour us a glass of wine, Martin, and come and have something to eat. Have you eaten at all today? No, I thought not."

Only then did Day realise he could smell cooking. Lamb, he thought, wine, and herbs. His mood lightened.

"Lamb with aubergine and potato," explained Helen as she removed the pot from the oven.

"You're a Gift of God, Helen!" he said. "Now that you mention it, I'm starving."

They took the food onto the balcony, together with two glasses and a nice bottle of red wine from Nemea. It was still relatively early in the evening, the air was warm and smelled sweetly of the dying grasses of the valley. From the hills they could hear the delicate but discordant chiming of goat bells. Day got to work with the corkscrew.

"You're right that I need to let Andreas do his job," admitted Day after his first sip. "I'll call him this evening. With luck he'll solve the Taygetus Raid and recover the stolen items. I've got a fairly good idea where he should look."

"You don't sound very pleased about it, Martin."

"I am, it's just that what I really want is to find out who killed Ricky Somerset, and why. How is Ben going to move on with his life otherwise? The robbery is nowhere near as important in my view."

"Don't you think Sotiris Artsanos killed Ricky? Andreas does."

"Andreas might be right and I might be wrong."

Helen gave a laugh which struck him as odd.

"What?"

"Not for one moment, Martin Day, do you think that you're wrong. Not now, not ever!"

They enjoyed the setting of the sun, and silence settled on the valley when the small brown birds in the fruit tree below the balcony finally ceased their evening chatter. The gentle chill of October in Greece finally made them move inside. Day sat in the main room, his glass of Nemean red wine refilled and his laptop in front of him. It was time to find out why Ricky's name had resonated with Aristos, whose remarkable memory should not be ignored. He would work through the night if necessary.

He would make a start and call Andreas later.

His search of the local newspaper records having turned up nothing, he decided to give up on that and search instead among the British newspapers, using Ricky's name and any key words he could think of.

The name of Naxos was a poor keyword as it brought up the famous record company of the same name. He would have to be creative. He started with the Di Quercia Tower, all the place names on Naxos that he could think of, and then the Artsanos family.

Helen had gone to her room and the wine was nearly finished when Day thought about the photographs in Evangelia's house. He typed in Ricky's name and the word 'fisherman'. His success took him by surprise.

The report was dated nineteen years earlier and was in a small British local newspaper called 'The Test and Itchen Gazette'. It was apparently named after two rivers near Southampton, and was no longer in business.

SOUTHAMPTON BACKPACKER RECOVERS FISHERMAN'S BODY

A young British backpacker spending the summer in the Greek islands told last night of a traumatic experience, a fire at sea in which a man died in front of him.

Ricky Somerset, 22, a student of Creative Writing at the University of East Anglia, had been swimming off the beach of Naxos Island when there was a loud explosion and a fishing boat went up in flames. Ricky describes seeing the owner of the boat being blown back from the engine by the force of the blast and falling into the water, engulfed in flames.

Ricky, whose family live in Southampton, bravely swam to the aid of the man and, though not able to save him, successfully brought his body to shore. The fire was later described as a tragic accident caused by an old and inadequately maintained engine. The victim is believed to have inadvertently ignited the fumes from the old engine while smoking.

The rest of the article consisted of a comparison with another boat fire in Southampton harbour several years before, and Day learned nothing more about the Naxos drama. So, Ricky had lied about not having been to Naxos before. In fairness, it was an experience anyone would wish to forget, and Ben had said that Ricky preferred not to dwell on the past. All the same, Day wanted to know more. He tried to search the records of the local coastal rescue services, but the website told him that searches could not be made online. He considered calling the police but instead picked up his mobile and dialled Aristos.

"Martin? Is something wrong?"

"No, Aristo, sorry to call rather late, I just need to ask you something," said Day. "Do you remember saying that you thought Ricky Somerset's name sounded familiar?"

"The poor man who died in the fire? Yes."

Day was stopped in his tracks. He had just seen the terrible irony of the fact that Ricky had witnessed a fatal fire as a young man and had later been consumed by fire himself. He managed to go on.

"Apparently he *has* been to Naxos before. It was nineteen years ago, and he witnessed a fire on a fishing boat. The fisherman died. I wondered if that would jog your memory."

"That's it! I remember now. It was all people could talk about at the time and for weeks afterwards. There was a young man on holiday who was taking a swim when a boat burst into flames. The police said the engine was old and hadn't been maintained, and the fisherman had probably caused the explosion himself with a cigarette or match. Sadly, it was an accident waiting to happen. Ricky's name stuck in my memory because he was kept in hospital for several days, and Rania and I felt very sorry for him. He had dived for the body and brought it back to the shore; it must all have been traumatising."

"Do you know the name of the man who died? I found the story in a British newspaper and the article didn't say."

"No, sorry. Rania might remember."

"Thanks, Aristo. I owe you a decent bottle of wine."

"You're welcome," said Aristos. "*Kalinichta.*"

Day hung up and closed his mobile thoughtfully. There was no way he would be able to sleep now, so he might as well keep working. He cleared the search bar on the laptop and typed in the words Sifones and Naxos.

The abandoned village in the hills near Apeiranthos was described on several websites, and there were images too. He saw low stone houses and broken walls around which the grass grew high. There was an old church there called Agios Ioannis, St John. It was still standing, its weathered white dome resilient to the sun and the wind; some of its internal murals were still visible, he read. The only thing that he could not find was when the people had abandoned Sifones to the empty echo of the winds.

The mystery of Sifones's desertion reminded him of ancient Mycenae, which had also been abandoned so suddenly that archaeologists had found signs of a hasty flight, bowls still containing traces of food knocked over in the middle of what had once been a room. The people appeared to have left without warning and never returned, possibly due to marauding invaders, but there were no bodies found, no evidence of a battle. They had left behind them a puzzle for historians which had caused hundreds of years of scholarly dispute. Sifones, he thought, was like a miniature Mycenae, in that its houses and walls were unable to tell their story, its inhabitants gone, leaving questions in their wake.

Next he looked up the church that Evangelia had mentioned, Panagia Chrysopigi. It was a tiny, ruined structure just south of Apeiranthos, even older than Agios Ioannis in Sifones. In fact, one archaeologist had put forward the proposal that it might have been a Mycenaean tomb before becoming a church. Now it was little more than a pile of stones. It might still provide somewhere to hide stolen antiquities where nobody would ever look for them, but Day thought it was less promising than Sifones.

He decided to search both Sifones and Panagia Chrysopigi the next morning. He hoped that in one or other of them he would find more than a sense of history. Contrary to what he had promised Helen, he decided it was too late to call Andreas, so poured himself the last of the Nemean red and spent another hour deep in thought.

21

Day woke the next morning to the sound of a message arriving on his mobile. He grabbed it from the bedside table, noting that the room was light. He rolled onto his side and propped himself up to read the message from Aristos.

Rania had remembered the story of the fisherman who had died in the fire on his boat nineteen years ago. It had happened off the coast near Agios Prokopios. She remembered it because she used to buy fish from the fisherman's van, which he would park along the port road in Chora after a good catch. The name on the side of the van was 'Artsanos'.

Day checked the time, threw back the sheet and headed for the shower, switching on the iron as he went. After his shower he rescued a shirt from the balcony where his washing was drying, ironed it and dressed quickly, enjoying the fleeting warmth of the cotton against his back. Coffee next, and he found Helen already in the kitchen acting on the same thought.

"You seem to be in a hurry," she observed. Day was not usually energetic in the mornings, and the current glint in his eye was most definitely out of character at what was, for him, a very early hour.

"Things to do," he said happily. "I never got round to calling Andreas last night, it got too late, so I'm going to Chora. I'm hoping to lure him to a café to talk to me, it's infinitely preferable to the police station."

"Anything new?"

Helen could read him so easily, Day thought. This time, however, he felt like keeping his ideas to himself until he knew rather more, so he shook his head.

"OK if I take the car? I'm going on somewhere else when I've seen Andreas. Back in the afternoon."

"I'm not going anywhere. I'd have loved a swim in the sea but it's too windy today."

Only then did Day notice the weather. The wind was gusty and seemed to be getting stronger. The Meltemi. It might make his search of Sifones and the ruined church more difficult, but not enough to stop him. It might even keep hikers away.

He stood at the balcony railing with his coffee to enjoy the breeze in his hair. It had clearly rained in the night. He could feel the wind, the freshness and the caffeine rinsing away his lassitude, leaving his mind alert. He sent a text to Andreas announcing that he was heading to town to see him, take him for a coffee, and tell him various new things that had come to light. Not waiting for a response, he pocketed the mobile, picked up his jacket from the back of a chair, and left the house.

By the time he reached Chora the prevailing Meltemi wind had strengthened, covering the dull sea with white lace and throwing water over the causeway to the islet of Palatia on which the ancient Portara stood. The flags flying outside the Naxos Port Authority building were tearing at their halyards. The light was silvery, the clouds in the bright sky blown so hard they splayed out like the pattern on a mackerel, and the wet roads were the colour of spilt mercury. The only vessel moored along the harbour that was not bucking in the swell was a large private boat which only swayed in a dignified manner.

Observing the one-way system along the harbour road, Day found a parking place in the main square and abandoned the Fiat, feeling like a local. As he walked towards the station, Andreas emerged from the building and came towards him, waving in a rather more relaxed way than Day had expected.

"Your suggestion of coffee was most welcome, Martin. *Kalimera! Ti kaneis?* Let's go to Café Seferis, it's not far and the coffee's good."

They bent into the wind as they left the square, and when Andreas pulled open the door to Café Seferis every head turned. The customers soon lost interest again when the door had shut, protecting the cosy warmth inside. The aroma of coffee was almost overwhelming, and Day found himself exchanging a conspiratorial smile with Andreas, like two boys who should have been at school.

Day changed his usual coffee order in recognition of the weather, and asked for a large cappuccino. Andreas asked for his usual Greek coffee *sketo*, without sugar. He might otherwise have ordered an espresso, he said, but was in no rush to get back to the station.

They found a table where they could talk with a reasonable expectation of privacy, their words obliterated by the hum of voices and the sound of the coffee machines.

"So, you said you have news for me?" Andreas began.

Day regretted the haste with which he had sent his morning text, boasting of his own discoveries, because now Andreas was not going to offer any information of his own. Moreover, Day had to choose his words carefully or face Andreas's anger when he discovered that he had gone to question Evangelia.

"I have two bits of news. The first concerns the Taygetus robbery. Yesterday I spoke to a woman called Evangelia. She's married to the catering manager at the Literary Festival, you might remember him. She's also the sister of Kostas and Sotiris Artsanos."

Day had had plenty of practice telling a good narrative and it was an ability he drew on now. He moved his story along quickly, so that Andreas had no chance to protest at his habit of meddling in police investigations.

"Evangelia knows all about Sotiris's criminal life. He has control over her and she can't stand up to him. She knew about the Taygetus robbery, and about the bronze horse hidden in the Di Quercia Tower. I told her to come to the police station and tell you what she knows in exchange for protection from her brother."

Andreas raised a hand, and it was impossible to ignore. Day stopped. Limiting himself to a stern glance, Andreas called the station and gave instructions that Evangelia was to be detained if she arrived before his return.

"So, let me see if I understand, Martin. You spoke to this woman *casually*, and she happened to say that her brother is a thief and she knows where he hides the stuff, and that she herself effectively stole one of the items for herself?"

"She was upset and frightened at the thought of her brother's anger. I calmed her down and offered her a way out, telling her she would get protection from the police. So yes, she opened up to me."

Andreas raised his eyebrows fractionally as he decided to swallow what he had been about to say.

"What exactly does this woman know about the Taygetus robbery?"

"I'm not sure she knows anything about the robbery itself. She knows that her brother uses the Di Quercia Tower to hide stolen antiquities, and she likes to look at them when he's away. As children they used to play round the tower and they all knew about the hiding place. Recently she took a special liking to the bronze horse and took it home with her, but she put it back afterwards for fear of her brother's anger. In the meantime, though, he had moved the haul to a new hiding place. Evangelia left the horse in the cellar hoping her brother would believe it had fallen out of the bag.

"We can be fairly sure when Evangelia went to the tower to return the horse. She didn't expect to find Nick Kiloziglou there taking some photographs, but he remembers her. They spoke together and he showed her round. Nick recognised her when he saw her again at the reception after Helen's lecture."

Andreas raised his chin and waited for Day to continue.

"I think we can guess where the rest of the goods might be hidden, Andrea. The Artsanos family grew up in a place called Sifones, which is an abandoned village in the hills near Kinidaros. The empty houses there would provide good hiding places, and Sotiris must know the place well. It's possible the stolen objects are still there."

"Did the woman tell you this too?"

"In a way."

"I'll arrange a police search. Is there anything else? I should be at the station when Artsanos's sister arrives."

"There's one more thing. It's worth hearing. Ricky Somerset told me he'd never been to Naxos before, but that was a lie. About two decades ago he came here as a student backpacker and was involved in an accident where a man died. Apparently Ricky was taking a swim off the beach at Prokopios when a fishing boat's engine exploded, and he saw the fisherman become engulfed in flames and fall into the sea. Ricky brought the body back to shore. It was in the British press."

Andreas looked shocked. "Death by fire, two cases of it, with Ricky Somerset involved in both. What's your theory, Martin? I know you must have one."

"Nothing good enough to tell you yet. But I discovered the name of the fisherman who died in the boat fire. The name was Artsanos."

Andreas sat back and combed his fingers through his mane of fair hair. Day suddenly noticed that Andreas had dark eyelashes, in stark contrast to the hair on his head. He noticed this because Andreas was blinking in surprise.

"Artsanos?" the policeman said, almost to himself. "Who in that family died twenty years ago?"

Day shrugged. Andreas excused himself and left the café like a man with an investigation to conduct.

Day finished his coffee, put some money on the table for their drinks and was blown back to his car. The wind was stronger than ever. The ringing of the wind in the rigging among the yachts moored along the quay was insistent, and took Day straight back to childhood holidays in the south of France when his mother was still alive. It was odd how enduring childhood memories could be, he thought, and smiled when he realised he also remembered the colour of his mother's summer dress. This reminiscence lasted him all the way to the car.

It was lunchtime but Day again had no appetite. He couldn't wait for Andreas, who was not the only one with an investigation to conduct. Day was completely focussed now on the abandoned village and the tomb-church, in one of which he hoped to discover a cache of stolen antiquities worth an unimaginable amount, if indeed a value could be put on them. More to the point, he hoped to find articles of great beauty and rarity such as he had spent much of his life studying and admiring.

22

Day studied his detailed map of Naxos while sitting in his car out of the wind. Sifones lay north of Apeiranthos and was relatively accessible by road, whereas the church of Panagia Chrysopigi was much more difficult to reach and further from the Di Quercia Tower. In Sotiris's position, Day would choose Sifones. He refolded the map meticulously and threw it on the passenger seat.

He drove through Agkidia, Halki and Moni, heading north. Once he had left the coastal area, the car was far less buffeted by the wind, and after Halki it barely seemed a force at all. High above, however, the sky was stormy, pelted with dark cloud behind which a serene blue sky occasionally shone.

He was about five kilometres north of Apeiranthos on the country road when he made out the dome of an old church to the west. He found a flat piece of ground off the road and parked the car. He could see a large number of low stone buildings among the hummocky grass beyond the church. He had read online that they were small farms that had been owned by people from nearby Koronos village, who at some point had abandoned them and left their lives in Sifones behind. Another article called Sifones a leper colony, but as there was only a single reference to this, Day found it hard to believe.

The view beyond the old village was dominated by more peaks than he could count, their edges starkly outlined in the washed, wind-driven sky. He set off along a path that led from the road downhill towards the deserted village. On all sides he was surrounded by scrub in every shade of green and gold, known in Greece as *maquis*, and a tangled carpet of ochre grasses. It was a truly stunning place, timeless and expansive, bounded only by the mountains and the sky. As he walked across the uneven ground towards the church, he peered into the empty buildings that he passed, single storey houses with no doors or windowpanes, grass growing in their front rooms, wooden lintels sagging over the windows. Weeds grew in every crevice. Many of the buildings had sturdy and very lovely arches over their doorways, and inside several of the houses he saw an arch between two rooms. He seemed to remember reading that these arches were a feature of this period in the Aegean. He picked his way carefully, wary of tripping or stumbling. In his mind he revisited the site of ancient Mycenae, a place abandoned for many more years than Sifones but which always filled him with the same sense of eery desertion.

He decided to start with the old church. Its exterior was in a poor state, the white cement cladding breaking away in places and grey with neglect. The iron doors with the cross design in the centre had been painted white, but not recently. He opened one and went inside, realising that the door opened easily, suggesting that other people also came here. Inside, as his eyes grew accustomed to the poor light, he made out a fresco which still faintly showed its original colours. He knew he would find no stolen antiquities here. A besom broom was propped against the wall for the use of anyone who wished to remove the leaves from the Lord's house, and little icons and a candle in a niche in the wall suggested recent if sporadic attendance.

A gust of wind hit him as he emerged from the church as if it had followed him from the coast. He looked round at the abandoned houses and the untended fields. Further away he saw sheep which undoubtedly belonged to some genuine shepherd, unlike their friend Sotiris Artsanos. As he was thinking of shepherds he noticed a long piece of wood like a shepherd's staff and picked it up. Even at this time of year there could be snakes in this grass, so he would use the stick to make a noise that would scare them away. So doing, he began to make a search of the houses.

He quickly realised what an impossible task he had taken on. It was a fool's mission, he thought, becoming increasingly frustrated. In these empty rooms there was nowhere to conceal anything, and there were hundreds of them.

He came to one house that seemed more promising. Although clearly abandoned for many years, there was a room that must have been a kitchen, with a large empty fireplace and some shallow niches in the wall for storing pots and pans. Day began to look round carefully. The room filled him with its sadness, a sadness inherent in anywhere that has been loved and lived in, and left behind. He found nothing and started to go back outside.

Something made him stop and listen: a foot on the path maybe, a movement of small stones, but the noise of the wind covered it and he decided he was mistaken. Outside he saw no-one, only the sheep which had come a little closer.

He took a path which seemed to lead back towards his car; it was overgrown with weeds and young scrub, ragged fig trees and neglected pomegranates. He looked into each building he passed, but these were even more decrepit than the ones he had already searched. He came to a small group of cottages, or possibly a farm, where the foundations of the structures seemed to have subsided. It was as if the ground was absorbing them. Day's long stick was now useful to prevent him from falling in a pothole.

It was thanks to the stick that he found the cave, though cave was too grand a word. It was a natural hole in the rock barely a metre tall at its highest point and very easy to overlook, but the vegetation which had once grown over it was pushed off to one side. Day stuck his staff into the hole and felt resistance. He switched on the torch on his phone, but he could still make out nothing inside the cave. To reach in with his bare hand was to ask for a snake bite, something he did not relish. He hesitated.

Just as he was hesitating there was an unmistakable noise, incredible and alarming, like a hand-thrown firework set off too close. He had no sense where it had come from. A second shot followed. He dropped the staff in alarm, picked it up again and ran for the nearest building. He leaned panting against the wall and listened to the silence that pulsated with the beating of his heart. He strained to hear approaching footsteps but even when the wind subsided he heard only sheep bells.

He knew he should make a run for it to his car, but his legs carried him the other way. He ran back to the cave and thrust his hand inside. No snake, but a canvas bag which he pulled out. He sat back on the grass in surprise and opened the bag quickly, looking round to see if anyone was near. He saw enough of the contents to make him start running for the road, and he only stopped when a big man stepped out to block his way, a single-barrelled shotgun in his hands which he was pointing at Day.

His head pounding, Day said nothing. This could only be Sotiris Artsanos, not away from the island after all. The cards were all in his opponent's hands.

In a thick dialect, the man with the shotgun asked who he was. It was better than being shot.

Day told him he was a friend of Evangelia.

"My sister told me about you," the man said coldly. "You're no friend of hers and you've taken a big risk."

"Not as big as the risks you take, Artsanos."

The man laughed without humour. "Yet it is I who am holding the shotgun and it's pointing at you. A tragedy is going to happen in a few minutes. I am here to shoot a rabbit for my favourite dinner, *kouneli stifado*, which I cook particularly well, although you will never taste it. Today there will be an unfortunate accident. I could not possibly have known you were here. You will be killed outright. That, I think, will be the end of my problem, don't you agree? Now put down the bag, I don't want your blood on it."

Day slowly lowered the canvas bag to the grass at his feet. He was planning to run to the church, the nearest refuge, though he had little hope of reaching it. Then Sotiris Artsanos turned his head away sharply with a look of shock on his face. It was Artsanos who then ran towards the church. A group of police, led by a fair-haired man in civilian clothes, were fast covering the ground from the road. Behind them, Day could see three police cars.

He sat down heavily where he stood, the bag at his feet, and bent his head over his knees. He began to laugh, uncertain exactly why.

"Martin? Are you hurt?"

"Andrea, I've never been so pleased to see anyone." He grinned at his friend and gave another stupid laugh before managing to control himself.

"What's in the bag?" said Andreas, reaching for it.

"Stolen goods, I imagine. I hope you're not going to arrest me for possession."

"I'd love to arrest you! How bloody stupid …"

A burst of shots from the church interrupted him but seemed to give Andreas no cause for concern. An officer came out with the shotgun broken over his arm, followed by the other policemen with Sotiris Artsanos in handcuffs.

Andreas helped Day to stand up.

"Are you safe to drive? If not, we'll bring your car and you can ride with me. You need to come to the station directly."

"I'm OK to drive. I'll follow you."

Day waited while the police pulled more bags from the small cave and prepared to return to Chora. He drove carefully and slowly after the police vehicles, soon falling behind and losing sight of them. He was surprised he'd been allowed to drive at all. He took the same road back as he had come, then on through Filoti and towards Halki. Somewhere after Halki he pulled in and rested his head on the steering wheel. It was some time before he felt like moving.

An inevitable and reasonable reaction, he thought, his eyes closed, and one that he preferred to deal with alone.

By the time he strode into the police station in Chora, Day was completely in possession of himself again. He made a statement and waited for the time when Andreas would speak to him privately. He anticipated a rigorous dressing-down.

He was shown to the only room in the station suitable for the man in charge, usually the office of the Naxos Chief of Police, Inspector Cristopoulos. Today the more senior man, Andreas himself, sat behind the large desk and waved Day to a chair.

"Take a seat, Martin."

"Before I forget to tell you, Andrea, you might find more stolen items hidden in the church of Panagia Chrysopigi near Danatos. Evangelia mentioned it, and of course I have no intention of looking …"

"I should hope not. I despair of you, Martin, but I realise that nothing I say will have any effect at all. It wasn't a coincidence that my men were on hand to 'save the day' at Sifones, you know; I guessed you'd go alone. When the woman didn't come to the station, it was clear that she had no intention of seeking our help. She betrayed you. You were lured into a trap by the brother and sister, and you made it easy for them."

"Will one apology suffice, Andrea?"

Andreas grunted.

"Are you going to arrest Evangelia?"

"She certainly has some questions to answer, not least what part she played in this afternoon's attempt on your life. Sotiris Artsanos killed Ricky, I'm certain of it: this afternoon proves him quite capable of murder. I can see you disagree, but you have to be reasonable. Why look for complications when the answer is staring you in the face?"

When Day did not reply, Andreas narrowed his eyes and folded his arms over his chest. He allowed the silence to lengthen, surprised that for once Day had nothing to say. He found it slightly disconcerting.

"May I just explain my thinking, Andrea?" said Day at last. "Let's take a step back. Two things preceded the murder in the past few weeks: the decision to restore the Di Quercia Tower and the start of the Naxos Literary Festival. Those two things not only preceded but *precipitated* what followed. We now know that the imminent building work on the tower forced Sotiris Artsanos to move his stolen goods from the tower's cellar to a new hiding place. It also made his sister Evangelia attempt to retrieve the horse which she had previously stolen from her brother's cache and returned to the hiding place. We know that the Literary Festival brought Ricky Somerset back to Naxos, and that his visit was complicated by his earlier role in the tragic death of a member of the Artsanos family. That's a link between Ricky and Sotiris Artsanos, even though it's circumstantial, that we can't ignore."

Andreas unfolded his arms and sat back in his chair with an air of vindication. His voice carried conviction.

"Sotiris Artsanos will confess to killing Ricky Somerset and starting the fire to destroy any evidence, I'm sure of it. Sometimes the answer really is in plain sight, I promise you. Ricky had become a threat to Artsanos, but whatever the truth is, we'll get it out of him."

"I don't see Sotiris as the murderer, Andrea."

"Don't be absurd, Martin, he tried to shoot you only this afternoon."

"He told me he would claim my death was a hunting accident. He had no plan to hide, or destroy the evidence. Whoever killed Ricky had a very different mind-set. For a Greek to start a fire in these tinder-dry conditions suggests some very strong motivation. The key to all this is not in the robbery, or even the murder, it's in the fire."

23

Andreas and Day faced each other across the desk, but Day no longer feared his ideas would be dismissed again. He could see Andreas's interest had been aroused.

"I don't think our paths are so very far apart, Martin. The details can be ironed out when our suspect is interrogated, but my point of view is supported by fresh evidence."

"Oh really?" At last, Day thought, two-way traffic.

"We've done some investigating of our own while you were busy looking for buried treasure. The Artsanos who died in the boat fire and sold fish from a van in Chora was one Manolis Artsanos. He was the father of Sotiris, Kostas and Evangelia."

"Are you suggesting that Sotiris killed Ricky because twenty years ago he pulled his father's dead body to shore for a decent burial? Does that really work?"

Andreas ignored him. "Sotiris's car matches the description given by the witness who reported two men arriving at the Di Quercia Tower in a vehicle and only one of them driving away."

"OK."

"Ricky's mobile phone is missing, it wasn't on the body. It would have betrayed his association with Sotiris, making it vital that Sotiris took it and destroyed it. We've questioned the other brother, Kostas, but he has a good alibi for the murder: he was working at his bar and many witnesses support that. Besides, he has no reason to kill Ricky Somerset, whereas the brother with a cache of stolen antiquities to protect is another matter."

Day shrugged, no longer following Andreas's argument very closely.

"Fair enough. You're the expert. Anyway, I promised Helen I'd leave the police work to you."

Day rose to leave and Andreas walked with him looking somewhat smug. Whether this was because he had won the argument or because Helen had been mentioned, only he knew. Before they reached the door, however, Day turned.

"Would you allow me a suggestion?" he said. "I want you and I to go together and talk to Evangelia's husband, Adonis Galanis."

For a moment Day was certain that Andreas would simply refuse. Any other policeman on the planet would surely have done so. This particular officer was of a different kind.

"Oh God. You'd better sit down again, Martin. I'm not inclined to embark on one of your mad schemes without a very good reason, but you know how much I enjoy your narratives."

Day sat down again in front of the Chief of Police's desk and marshalled his thoughts. Hearsay and supposition being all that he had, the best he could do was paint a good picture. Across the large desk Andreas was staring at him somewhat fiercely.

"Before you begin, Martin, why shouldn't I conclude you're still in shock after what happened this afternoon?"

"This isn't an emotional reaction. I've been thinking this through and you should hear it. The first time I met Adonis was at a Festival event when Athina introduced him to me; he's a particularly good-looking guy. One of my friends later commented that if she hadn't met his wife she would have guessed Adonis was gay. I didn't make anything of that at the time, but one of the writers remarked that Ricky had been flirting with Adonis. He said it was obvious that something was going on between them, so much so that everyone at the Festival knew about it."

"Where exactly are you going with all this?"

"Wait a minute. It could explain the conflicting reports of Ricky's plans for the day he died. Ricky told Ben that he'd find his own way home some time later, making the excuse of a group excursion somewhere. He told the other writers that Ben was picking him up for a nice evening meal. I think both Ben and the writers have told the truth, and that it was Ricky himself who was lying."

He paused for effect, as he habitually did in making his historical documentaries. Andreas avoided giving him the satisfaction of a prompt to continue. It was too early to look interested.

"I think Ricky was fascinated by Adonis. Ricky was an artist, openly and proudly gay, but Adonis, a married man with a respectable position, had to be discreet. That didn't stop Ricky. Ben described Ricky to me as a person who wanted to experience as much as he could in life and not look back. Loyalty to Ben perhaps counted for little in such a world view. Let's say for now that Ricky wanted to see rather more of Adonis's beauty."

"If we must," muttered Andreas.

"Ricky flirts with him and possibly even offers him money. Adonis is in need of money - wife, small house, two tiny incomes. Adonis agrees to take Ricky to the desolate Di Quercia Tower after the Saturday session of the Festival, which ends at two o'clock, and Ricky arranges to be free. The scene is set for Ricky and Adonis to leave together unobserved, with hours of freedom to enjoy."

"You're suggesting they went to the Di Quercia Tower in Adonis's car?"

"Exactly! I've seen Adonis's car, and it's the same as so many others - mine, Ben's, probably Sotiris's - most of the hired and secondhand cars on Naxos, in fact. Your witness saw Adonis's car, and the men who got out of it were Ricky and Adonis."

"And only Adonis drove it away…"

"Yes, but you're leaping ahead. They arrive at the tower and do whatever they've agreed to do in some private area, my guess is the cellar. Adonis already knows the tower well because Evangelia has taken him there. Afterwards they see the scaffolding and decide to climb it for the view. The proverbial post-coital smoke, metaphorically speaking. I don't know what happens at the top, whether he trips or is pushed, but Ricky falls from the top to the bottom of the tower. I suppose that Adonis left as quickly as he could, which your witness confirms."

"And the fire?"

"I don't know. I really have no idea yet."

Andreas pushed his chair back from the desk, stretching his legs out as if it might ease the tension in his imagination.

"As usual you tell a good story, my friend, but it poses a great many unanswered questions and involves too much guesswork. Not least, you assume that a happily married man is willing to take part in a physical homosexual relationship for cash ..."

"Never heard of bisexuality, Andrea?"

"Another unproven assertion, Martin."

"At least say you'll come with me and talk to him."

"Who suggested you would have a role in this?"

"Come on, Andrea. When he sees me Adonis will know I spoke with his wife and haven't been silenced by his brother-in-law, and he'll be worried about what Evangelia might have told me about him. I'll talk him into an admission of guilt."

"What a load of rubbish," said Andreas, but Day saw that he was trying not to smile. His case was won.

24

That evening Helen suggested dinner at Taverna O Thanasis. She had spent the day working on an idea for a new book, and had given no thought to food; she was not even sure they had anything at all in the house.

"We must go to the supermarket tomorrow," she remarked.

"Tomorrow might be difficult for me," said Day, wondering where to start to bring her up to date. It was an excellent idea to eat at the taverna, because over dinner he could take his time to explain. "Maybe we could eat at Thanasis's for a few nights till we can go and buy food. Vital supplies like milk are easy to pick up in the village."

Realising that it would be Helen who would have to do the picking up of vital supplies, he hastened to change the subject.

"Just give me half an hour to shower and change, and we can go."

They separated to their different rooms, and Day washed away the actual and metaphorical dust of his adventure in Sifones. He chose a favourite shirt, ran the iron over it, and dressed rather more smartly than usual. After all, he could reasonably consider this evening as a celebration of having avoided becoming the victim of a hunting accident.

He stupidly made some such remark on emerging, and Helen whirled round.

"What do you mean, you were nearly used as target practice?"

It was a gusty walk to the village, but Day enjoyed something as natural as the force of the wind on his face; his mind felt clogged. They found a quiet table inside against the wall, and he looked frankly at Helen.

"I'm sorry, Helen. I'm sorry I haven't shared very much with you recently. It's probably because I know you don't think I should get involved in these things. You're absolutely right, but I can't seem to avoid it."

"I think you take unnecessary risks. Today, for example."

"Fair enough. Anyway, may I tell you everything that's happened recently? I wouldn't mind hearing your thoughts on it all. You have a way of seeing things that I miss."

"I doubt you miss much, Martin."

"Ah, sadly I do," he laughed. "A few days ago you reminded me that to err is human, and it turns out I'm actually human! I went to examine a *krater* in the Naxos Museum that I thought was a match with one in the British Museum, but in fact I was completely wrong.

That was quite a shock."

"That doesn't happen very often to you, and don't go blaming it on getting older. You're not even forty yet. Not for a few weeks anyway!"

Day laughed. "The trick is not to make mistakes when it really matters, I suppose. Ah, here comes Thanasis."

"Good evening, Martin, good evening Helen, it's been too long since we saw you."

This was accompanied by an unusual amount of handshaking and double kisses. They had clearly been missed. Day was pleased to be back, especially as he had developed an outstanding appetite.

"Now, what does your clever wife have in the kitchen today?" he asked.

"Today she has some excellent veal," said Thanasis, turning up his face as he spoke as if to enjoy the warmth of the sun. "So, there is grilled veal chop, or a tasty Veal with Eggplant - or aubergine, as I think the British call it. Or there is a Veal *Kelaidi*."

Day and Helen exchanged a glance but clearly neither had heard of this before.

"*Kelaidi* is a dish from Northern Greece, near Larissa. My wife's sister lives there and gave her this recipe. A small heap of tender veal shoulder is placed in a dish and covered with layers of onion, tomato and green pepper. It is cooked slowly, then topped with Feta or Kefalotyri cheese, which is allowed to melt over the *kelaidi* in the oven." He lowered his voice. "The secret ingredients are melted butter and a lot of garlic!"

Since there was clearly no possibility of choosing anything else, Helen asked what Thanasis recommended to accompany the *kelaidi*.

"Ah, La Belle Helene!" he beamed. "For you and Martin I propose the *patates fournou* - our finest Naxian potatoes roasted with olive oil and oregano - and then something simple and clean for the palate, such as a salad of cabbage and carrot. You know this? It is raw sliced vegetables softened in salted water, rinsed well, and dressed with oil and lemon juice. Delicious, and very healthy!"

Despite the substitution of roast potatoes for his beloved chips, Martin had to agree that this was a meal worthy of the occasion. With a small bow and another smile at Helen, Thanasis departed for the kitchen.

He returned within minutes carrying a tray. He placed a small bottle of ouzo, a jug of cold water and a bowl of ice cubes on the table, and added a small dish divided into three which held olives, slices of sweet pepper and delicate cubes of hard cheese.

"The food will be a little while, my friends, so please enjoy a little ouzo on the house while you're waiting."

Day brought the tray closer to him, placed a chunk of ice in each glass and added a measure of the clear distilled liquid. The ouzo began to turn cloudy on contact with the ice. He handed one to Helen, who added a little water. The aroma of aniseed brought a smile to their faces.

"Cheers."

"*Stin yia sas!*"

"Perhaps we should toast the person who turned out to be a bad shot and didn't take your head off today," said Helen.

"It wasn't that close. He never even tried to fire at me. He just threatened to."

"I'm not sure that makes me feel much better, Martin. Perhaps you would start at the very beginning? We have all evening."

Before the arrival of the veal, Day managed to summarise his visit to Evangelia and his subsequent conversation with Andreas. He was pleased that Helen chose not to interrupt during his story, but slightly apprehensive that the cross-questioning afterwards could be searching. Eventually he was forced to ask.

"I thought you would say something. Why are you so quiet?"

"I'm thinking," she said. "Go on."

He resumed the story, receiving a critical glance at the point where he left home for Sifones without telling her where he was going. The Sifones adventure, as he had come to call it, evoked satisfying gasps of horror from Helen, and one 'My God!'.

"I'm amazed that Andreas let you get away with that. I imagine he told you not to have any more to do with the case?"

"The opposite, in fact," Day fibbed in the interest of brevity. "Tomorrow we're going to confront Adonis Galanis together."

"Why? Why on earth are *you* doing that, Martin? Oh never mind, I know you better than to expect a sensible answer. Andreas is definitely going to be there, isn't he?"

"Of course, and with quite a few police to be on the safe side." He told her about his theory that Adonis had been with Ricky at the time he fell from the Di Quercia Tower.

"Actually, I agree with you about Adonis. He reminds me of the myth of Narcissus, the beautiful young man who fell in love with his own reflection in the water, but was so eager to kiss the face that he loved that he fell into the water and drowned. Foolish and self-destructive."

"I think I know what you mean. I remember your laugh when you first saw Adonis."

"That was rude of me. He's just so impossibly beautiful…"

"It appears Ricky Somerset may have thought so too."

The door to the kitchen opened and a procession came towards their table. It consisted of the short figure of Koula bearing a dish of meat, and her son Vangelis following with two more platters. She put the plate of veal in the centre of their table without saying a word, which made more impact than anything she could have said. The melted cheese was glistening as it enfolded the two stacks of vegetables and meat, the scent of garlic was pungent, and the liquid on the floor of the dish bore out Thanasis's promise of melted butter.

"That looks wonderful!" said Day, then remembered that the lady spoke no English so repeated it in his most flowery Greek with a few extra embellishments, which made both mother and son laugh.

Vangelis had only to say the word 'wine' and, at Day's grin, returned with a jug of red from the barrel and two glasses. The feast was set. Day poured Helen some wine, then himself, and they began to help themselves to the food. He raised his glass in another toast.

"To the amazing Koula!"

"To Koula."

They spoke about nothing other than their meal while they ate. It would have been deeply wrong not to give the food their full attention. When little remained but some cabbage salad, Helen began to talk, but not about Day's adventures. She described some ideas for a story inspired by the positive effect of the Literary Festival. She asked after Athina and that young lady's interest in Day; and, thrown in casually, she told him of her gentle refusal of another invitation to dinner from Andreas.

Having enthused about the novel and smiled noncommittally about Athina, Day found nothing to say about the last piece of information. It was his turn to be surprised.

They walked home and Helen made herself a cup of tea. Day poured himself a glass of water and sat down on one of the dining room chairs, his feet propped on the rungs of another.

"Are you ready to give me your thoughts?" he asked her. "I meant it when I said I value your opinion."

"Not yet. All I can tell you is that I think there are more layers to this onion than you've uncovered yet. A catalogue of errors, perhaps."

Day smiled. "I do all the leg work and you see into the heart of the matter," he said lightly. "We should get together."

25

Day surprised himself by managing to leave the house the next morning at half past six. He even felt alert and excited, no trace of the usual malaise which often hung round him at such an hour. The wind of the previous day had disappeared, and there was virtually no traffic on the road between Filoti and Chora until he reached the port area and encountered delivery vans visiting the restaurants and tavernas with supplies of fresh produce. He parked close to the police station and breezed into the reception area.

Andreas was already there giving instructions to four officers, all of whom were armed. As usual Andreas was not in uniform, but there could be little doubt of who was in charge.

"Good morning, Martin. Men, *Kyrie* Day will be with us today as a permitted civilian. You have your instructions. Let's get going."

A patrol car and police van were standing ready in front of the station, and Day got into the back of the car with Andreas. From the corner of his eye he saw Inspector Cristopoulos leaving the station after them but he was soon lost to sight. Their vehicle led the way out of Chora and took Day's usual route towards the inland villages, heading for Apeiranthos.

"When we reach the house it's important you remember I'm in charge, Martin. The suspect may turn violent, and most people in the rural areas have some kind of weapon."

"There's a shotgun in the main room," Day confirmed.

"Right. All the more reason to let my men do their job. Once the place is secure, you may question the man or the woman if you believe you can be instrumental in getting the truth from them. However, you must do whatever I say, without fail, for everyone's safety. Understood?"

"Absolutely."

"Good."

At Apeiranthos, Day was asked to direct the driver to the house. He was then instructed to remain on the street while the police entered the building, and when he was called in he saw Adonis and Evangelia sitting at their kitchen table with police behind them. One of the officers had taken charge of the shotgun.

Adonis was angry and demanded to be told the reason for the arrival of armed police in his home. He was expected at work at nine o'clock, he told them.

"That's why we've called on you this early," said Andreas calmly. "We wouldn't want to miss you. We have some questions about the death of Ricky Somerset."

He allowed his gaze to fall on the photographs on the wall as if deep in thought, before focussing his glare upon Adonis.

"We believe, *Kyrie* Galanis, that you were present at the Di Quercia Tower when Ricky Somerset died. I strongly urge you to tell us the truth now, for your own sake. Lying will only make things worse for you."

Adonis said nothing, but his calculating stare shifted from Andreas to Day. This was all the excuse Day needed.

"You know the Di Quercia Tower very well," he said firmly. "Your wife and her siblings played in it as children, and she must have taken you there many times. Your wife told you that the restoration was due to start, and then that the scaffolding had been completed. Thinking that nobody would be working at the weekend, you took Ricky there."

"I don't have anything to say to you," muttered Adonis, traces of the local dialect now evident in his speech.

"Then I'll do the talking. You'd managed to get a responsible and well-paid job at the Festival. You must have been glad of the income. *Kyrie* Bazeos pays fairly and looks after his staff. So perhaps you didn't want to know, at first, when one of the guests made passes at you. The other guests were starting to notice, and you were afraid you might lose your job. Correct so far?"

The man stared him out. Day was surprised at the coldness that filled the handsome face. He went on as if completely at ease.

"Ricky Somerset was not to be put off. He had made up his mind to have an adventure with you. He flattered you, offered you money, pressed you to give him what he wanted. When did you agree? How much persuasion did it take?"

Day noted that Evangelia had flushed and was staring at her hands, which were clasped in front of her on the table. He made a show of changing his mind.

"No, I see I have it the wrong way round. It was you who seduced Ricky. After all, Ricky was happy in his relationship with Ben Lear, Ricky had no need to take a risk. But you saw a chance to make some money and indulge the side of you that you keep hidden most of the time. And at some point Ricky decided to go along with it and have a fling with one of the best-looking men in Greece."

"Nothing like that happened," said Adonis, breaking his silence.

"I think it did. Ricky as good as told me so himself. He set up elaborate excuses to go off with you. He told his husband not to pick him up that afternoon saying he was going out with a few friends, and he told his friends that Ben was collecting him as normal. He was setting the stage for you to slip off together unhindered. Which is exactly what you did. What car do you own?"

Adonis's reluctance to answer was reversed by an imperious gesture from the policeman behind his chair.

"Fiat 500. White."

"Indeed. You drove Ricky to the Di Quercia Tower in your car as soon as you could both leave the Festival unobserved. As it was Saturday people left promptly at two o'clock because the rest of the day was free time; I guess you got away about half past two. You were seen arriving at the Di Quercia Tower soon afterwards. You parked near the tower and you both got out. Why don't you tell the inspector what you did next?"

"He was running the show," said Adonis in a low voice. He shifted in his seat to look at his wife but she kept her eyes down. "Okay, we went to the tower, and you're right, money was promised, but I never saw any of it. Ricky loved the cellar, he said he could feel all the secrets of the old place. What we did didn't take long. Afterwards he wanted to look round the tower. It was he who insisted on climbing up the scaffolding to stand on the parapet."

Adonis stopped and bit at the skin around his thumbnail abstractedly. Day was aware that Andreas was focussing intently on the next part of the story.

"What happened at the top?" Day prompted.

"I didn't see. We were standing at different parts of the parapet. One minute Ricky was leaning against the wall shielding his eyes with his hand, looking out. The next minute he was gone. I heard him land on the ground below."

"What did you do then?"

"I thought he'd jumped. I ran to where he'd been standing and could see him on the ground. His mobile was right there on the wall, so I took it; I knew it would connect us. I climbed down the scaffolding and went to Ricky, but he was dead. I panicked. I ran back to the car and drove away. I knew there was nothing I could do for Ricky, and … and I wanted to protect Evangelia."

Andreas snorted, but said nothing. It was as eloquent as any sentence.

"And the mobile? Where is it now?"

"In the sea."

"There was clear evidence of a struggle having taken place on the edge of the parapet where Ricky went over," Andreas said harshly. "How do you account for that? Ricky didn't fight with himself."

"You're wrong," Adonis said eventually. "There was no struggle."

"Perhaps there was … intimacy?" suggested Day.

Andreas lost patience. "What about the fire, Galanis? Did you start it? I want to know about the fire."

Andreas could be an intimidating man when he felt like it, Day thought. To Day he was awe-inspiring, but to Adonis Galanis he was probably terrifying.

"There was no fire when I left. I swear!"

It had the ring of truth and Andreas grunted and let it go. He ordered his men to handcuff Adonis but to keep him at the table. Evangelia watched with a pale face and moist eyes as her husband's hands were fastened behind his back and he was restrained in his seat. Andreas drew a chair from the table and sat opposite her. It was not a comforting gesture.

"*Kyria* Evangelia, did you know about your husband's sexual preferences before today? You don't seem completely surprised."

"Of course I knew. How could I not know? But I thought he'd managed to stop doing it, you know, which he promised me when we got married. I knew he found it hard. But I know he loves me!"

Tears fell down her face. Day thought they were genuine. Adonis appeared to be frozen in his chair.

"*Kyria*, are you saying that what your husband did was not purely for the money?" Andreas insisted.

Evangelia nodded. "He wanted it too. He has needs I couldn't satisfy."

"You're an unusually understanding wife. Did your husband tell you what happened at the tower that day?"

"Not at first. Later. He was in shock."

"I'm sure he was. What else did he tell you that he hasn't just told us?"

She shook her head, and Day could wait no longer. He and Andreas had talked on the drive from the police station, and it was time to put the plan into action.

He turned back to the husband.

"I think it's time we stopped pretending this was all about sex and money. This was a great deal more than a lust-driven assignation, wasn't it? You didn't just take a liking to Ricky Somerset at the Festival and see a chance to make some cash. You already knew him."

Day was pleased to see Adonis and Evangelia stiffen in their seats.

"You knew him from twenty years ago when Ricky came to Naxos on holiday as a student. His visit ended in tragedy with the death of Evangelia's father, Manolis Artsanos. I suspect that you weren't completely sure whether this successful writer was the same person as the student who pulled Manolis's body to the shore, so you took him to the Di Quercia Tower to find out, one way or the other. And don't waste time denying it, because it's true: it was indeed Ricky Somerset who played a part in the death of Manolis Artsanos."

Adonis appeared to come to a decision and nodded grimly, his eyes shining. "I recognised his name when I saw the list of Festival guests, but I wanted to be sure it was the same man. I wanted to confront him and have it out with him, so yes, I flirted with him and took him to the tower that day to force him to tell me the truth."

"And what did he tell you?"

"He didn't say much. I told him that I'd actually witnessed what happened to Manolis that day. I was on the beach, you see. Ricky was *in* the boat with Manolis before the explosion. I watched Ricky jump overboard to save himself. They'd been arguing. It looked to me as if they were having some kind of fight. That could even have been how the fire in the boat started. At the time he was called a hero for bringing Manolis's body to shore, but I knew what really happened. I couldn't say anything at the time, nobody would have believed me, I was only fifteen. I was just starting to go out with Evangelia. So when I had Ricky at the tower I demanded the truth."

"So," insisted Andreas, "you fought with Ricky on the parapet and threw him over the edge."

"No, I swear. He just fell."

Andreas signalled to his men to take Adonis out, which they did without much gentleness. When calmness returned to the room Day expected to see Evangelia in tears again. Instead, she was white-faced and dry-eyed with shock.

"Do you have anything to add, *Kyria?*" said Andreas more gently than before. The woman shook her head. "Your husband will be taken to the police station in Chora and charged. If you want to add anything to what you've told us, go there and ask for me, Inspector Nomikos."

Andreas made to leave and gestured Day to precede him. Day shook his head mutely. Andreas nodded and left.

Day turned back to the table and sat in the chair Andreas had just vacated, facing Evangelia.

"You and I haven't finished," he said, "I want to hear the rest of it."

26

Evangelia said nothing. They heard the doors of the police van slamming and the voice of an officer telling onlookers to move away. The sound of vehicles leaving was followed by silence. Day and Evangelia sat opposite one another without a word.

Knowing what he knew, believing what he now believed, Day felt his breath become more shallow. His placed a mask of impassivity on his face and waited, saying nothing and staring directly at the woman. She looked surprised, as if she had expected his sympathy or words of comfort. Gradually the vulnerability left her face.

After several minutes she abruptly stood up and ordered him out of her house. Day told her to sit down. Somewhat to his own surprise, his voice had a nasty, vicious edge that he didn't recognise, and the woman did as he said. Again she fell silent, seemingly resolved to face him out.

"You've always intended your husband to take all the blame," began Day. "That way you could be rid of him and his sexual escapades. His lust for men must always have offended you, but he's also been useful, which is why you married him. He was your refuge from your violent brother Sotiris, and your pathway to respectability, which you've always craved. You saw a chance to be rid of both your brother and your husband at the same time, with Adonis taking the blame for Ricky's death and Sotiris being charged with armed robbery. You could wash your hands of them and still pose as a respectable woman wronged by her family. People would eventually have sympathised with you."

"Has anyone ever told you that you're full of …"

A dialect word that Day had not heard before completed the insult, but her meaning was clear. He already knew this was a woman whose character was not as gentle as it seemed.

"I know what really happened on the day Ricky died. I'm just curious about the details. What was your intention, for example, when you went to the Di Quercia Tower that afternoon? Did you already know what you were going to do?"

Evangelia shook her head and laughed in his face, all pretence of innocence a thing of the past.

"You don't know anything," she snapped.

"I know more than you imagine. For one thing, Adonis didn't see the fire on your father's boat from the beach: you did. You told him about it afterwards. Your father died horribly, and when you were fifteen it must have been agonising to watch. You hated Ricky from that moment, hated him enough to kill him twenty years later when he returned to Naxos."

It was Evangelia's face which had now become a mask. Day continued, confidently.

"I believe your husband does love you, and when he saw Ricky's name on the guest list at the Festival he saw an opportunity to please you, to confront the man whom you held responsible for your father's death. At the same time he could even satisfy his own sexual needs without fear of your anger. When Adonis told you what he was planning I expect he played down the sexual element and emphasised his intention to confront Ricky. All you needed to do was let Adonis carry out his plan and you might have found out Ricky's version of the truth. But that wasn't enough for you, was it? You were consumed by two powerful emotions - disgust at what your husband would be doing with Ricky, and an overwhelming need for revenge."

"You really don't know anything about it!" Evangelia shouted, and covered her face with her hands. Day wondered what expression they were now concealing.

"You planned to arrive at the Di Quercia Tower at the time Adonis had told you he would be there with Ricky. You went on foot, like you did when you went to retrieve the bronze horse. You were early, so you hid and watched your husband and Ricky arrive. Perhaps you heard them in the cellar. I do have some sympathy for you about that."

She took her hands from her face, and to Day's horror she was smiling. It was not a kind smile.

"You hid and waited," he continued. "I think by this time you had made up your mind to have your revenge, knowing that Adonis would be blamed and removed from your life. What did you do next, Evangelia?"

The smile broadened and the woman began to laugh, a cold laugh without humour, without reason. She began to nod as if she was about to tell him everything. After all, there were no witnesses to anything she told him.

"I watched my father die from the beach. I saw Ricky Somerset and my father wrestling in the boat, and Ricky diving into the sea just before the engine exploded. My father was covered in flames and shouting and then he fell over the side. Ricky just lay in the water. Ricky killed my father. He punched him, he started the engine fire, and he jumped into the sea to save himself.

"When Adonis told me that Ricky was back on the island and that he planned to confront him, I was going to leave it to Adonis. I was stunned, I wasn't capable of thinking clearly.

"Then a cleaner at the Bazeos Tower came to see me. Nasty woman, the type who loves stirring up trouble for other people. She'd come to tell me that my husband and one of the male guests were having a relationship, and that everybody knew about it. Adonis said it was just his way of getting close enough to Ricky to be able to find out what happened. He said he was doing it for me.

"That Saturday, Adonis told me he would be late home after the session at the Festival because he was taking Ricky to the Di Quercia Tower. He said he'd told Ricky that the tower would make a great setting for a story, but when they got there they'd be alone and he could force Ricky to tell him the truth. I knew there was more to it. I could feel Adonis's excitement.

"The tower is a special place to me, I go there all the time. It should have been my actual home, it used to belong to my mother's family. I know every path to it, every inch of it. Nobody saw me go there that afternoon. Adonis and Ricky were there when I arrived, they must have arrived sooner than Adonis told me. Our car was parked nearby. I saw them as they left the cellar and were starting to climb up the scaffolding to the parapet. They were laughing, laughing in such a way that I knew exactly what they'd been doing. I started to follow them. They were so involved in each other they didn't notice me. When I got to the top I saw Adonis and Ricky had started again, right there on the parapet. They were so wrapped up in each other they wouldn't have noticed a coach-load of tourists arriving.

"I flew at Adonis with my fists, hitting him as hard as I could, shouting, letting out all the feelings I'd been bottling up. Adonis turned away from me and I started on Ricky - well, can you blame me? I hit him and hit him and hit him."

"Which of you pushed Ricky off the tower?"

"Nobody did. We were right at the top, I suppose the men had found it exciting up there on the edge. The parapet wall is very low at that place. Ricky couldn't save himself when he lost his balance. It all happened so quickly. Adonis and I just watched him go over the edge."

"My God."

"Believe me, God was nowhere to be seen."

"What happened next?"

"We went down to the bottom and Adonis said that Ricky was dead. He wanted to get away as quickly as possible. He took the car and told me to go home on foot, as if returning from my usual walk."

She folded her arms, triumphant, like somebody recounting a success story. Day knew she had a major chapter still to tell.

"Tell me," he said. "did you feel better? Did Ricky's death feel sweet to you?"

"No."

"No, I didn't think so."

"What would you know about it?"

"I know about the fire, Evangelia."

He allowed the silence to lengthen, wondering how he could get the woman to tell him what happened next. He needed to hear it in her own words. He heaved an exaggerated sigh.

"You're right," he admitted. "Nobody saw what happened and nobody will ever know the truth. Everyone will think that Ricky fell from the tower by accident, which is pretty poor vengeance for your father."

"My father *is* avenged! My father died by fire, and so did the man who killed him. It was the perfect vengeance, the perfect punishment, and I made sure of that, even if nobody else would."

"If you say so, but we'll never know for sure."

Evangelia slammed both hands flat on the table in front of her and leaned towards him in fury. The torrent of abuse she released at Day was, mercifully perhaps, in the Cretan dialect which he found impossible to follow. Day glanced towards the door.

Seeing her outburst had not been understood, Evangelia was forced to repeat herself.

"Ricky Somerset died by fire, just like my father. Ricky caused the fire that burned my poor father alive, and I lit a fire over Ricky with dry leaves and sticks and set light to it using Adonis's lighter. *I* did it, *I* avenged my father. If *you* don't get it, Ricky certainly did! He watched me doing it. His body may have been broken, but he was still alive, and he knew what was happening. I made sure. I told him all about it before I set him alight."

"Christ!" said Day, a remark lost in the crash of the door as it was flung open by Andreas and his men. The officers handcuffed the furious Evangelia and took her out.

Day and Andreas looked at each other. Their plan had worked, but they had not anticipated the horror that had temporarily stolen from them the power of speech.

Andreas stretched out a hand and touched Day's arm, guiding him from the house and into the road. Just outside stood Inspector Cristopoulos with more officers, and two unmarked cars further down the street. The Naxos Police had come out in force.

Day handed Andreas the device on which Evangelia's confession had been recorded, and watched as the door of a police car closed on her.

27

He travelled back to Chora in the back seat of the police car with Andreas. Cristopoulos was in the front passenger seat, staring ahead as if unable to hear their conversation. There was not much that Day needed to say, as Andreas and Cristopoulos had been silently listening to everything from immediately outside the house. After a while they fell silent, thinking their own thoughts.

"There's nothing to keep me on Naxos once this case is closed," Andreas said out of the blue. "We should have a drink before I go."

"Let's do that."

"Better if it's just the two of us. Helen would probably prefer not to see me at the moment. It's better if I give it a little time."

"I see." An inadequate response, he chided himself, but the best he could think of. "It will be good to see you. Tomorrow? Text me."

Andreas nodded.

"I have a favour to ask you, Andrea. I'd appreciate seeing the stolen antiquities if possible. It's a chance in a lifetime for someone in my job."

Andreas considered the merit of the suggestion and it went in Day's favour.

"Fair enough, I think you've earned that. In fact, a correct assessment of exactly what Artsanos's share of the haul contains would be useful to us. Yes, we could make that tomorrow, if it suits you?"

At the police station Day got out, relieved he was being allowed to go straight home. Evangelia was being taken out of the police van watched by one or two passers-by. Andreas resumed command, preoccupied with his responsibilities, and disappeared into the station without looking back. Inspector Cristopoulos, however, looked round for Day and raised his hand in a small gesture of farewell. Day smiled, strangely touched.

He drove to Filoti thinking of what had happened, arriving with no recollection of the journey home. It was not even noon. Helen was out. He ate some cheese alone on the balcony then went to his room. Changing into stronger shoes he left the house and walked across the rough countryside for nearly three hours. When he reached the house again he called Ben.

"Have you heard from the police today, Ben?"

"No. Why?"

"They've arrested the two people responsible for Ricky's death. Shall I come over? I can tell you everything."

"Of course, oh my God!"

"I'll be there as soon as I can."

Day stopped only to change his shoes and leave a note for Helen. He drove to Paralia Votsala and pulled up outside the Elias House, where he paused to get a grip of himself. How he would have loved a few hours talking to Ben like they used to do, a conversation at least twenty-five years overdue. Instead he must somehow tell Ben what had happened. Better it came from a friend, but he was dreading it.

Day was quite good at delivering a narrative. It was an ability which had made him a successful presenter of history programmes on some pretty obscure subjects. That evening, however, he delivered his story to Ben in a halting, emotional, reluctant manner which none of his producers would have recognised.

He came to the end of Evangelia's confession and stopped. Ben would not be interested in whatever happened now to Evangelia and her husband. Day knew with appalling certainty that the image in Ben's mind was the picture of Ricky watching her as she built a bonfire around him.

"I can't think of anything I could possibly say ... I'm so sorry..."

"I needed the truth, Martin. It was brave of you ..."

Ben excused himself and left the room. The house was quiet, the other guests having gone, and Day could hear noises from upstairs that he wished he could not hear. He went outside to give Ben some privacy. The Meltemi wind had passed and normal weather had been resumed. It was the so-called golden hour, the time that photographers love. The sun was setting into the sea with an inappropriate flamboyance. He stood on the beach to watch. With an inevitability which brought reassurance, the red sun slowly changed shape as the straight line of the sea consumed it from the base. When the sun disappeared, the sky retained its colour and the sea became a black that was indescribably enriched with magenta.

He jumped, aware that Ben was standing behind him.

"Sorry, I didn't mean to startle you." His voice, normally so musical, was ragged.

"Are you okay?"

"No, but you know what? What I want to do now is go over there and raise some kind of toast to my brave Ricky."

Ben pointed to Taverna Ta Votsala on the far side of the bay. Hiding his surprise, Day nodded. He had no idea how going to a restaurant was right for Ben now, but it was Ben's call.

On their walk to the taverna, Day listened as Ben spoke of Ricky. He was prepared to listen all night, just as long as he was spared the need to say very much. He was bad at finding the right words to bring consolation. If things looked black to a friend, they always looked blacker to Day.

They took the furthest table on the beach near the sea, and the owner, Day's friend Vasilios, recognised Ben and sensed their need for privacy. He brought them two glasses of ouzo and a jug of water with the briefest of nods.

It was almost completely dark and quite cool now. The taverna lights glimmered on the water.

"If we spend all evening drinking to Ricky, that's fine by me. I don't need to get drunk, I just don't really know what else to do tonight. I appreciate the company, Martin."

"I can do company," he said.

"It's only four years since I first met Ricky."

Day muttered something about remembering the good times.

"Look, Martin, nothing you can say tonight is going to help me or hurt me, so just drink with me and listen to the rubbish I want to say. Okay? Really, I can't think of anyone else I'd rather have sitting in that chair tonight. Apart from Ricky."

Day reverted to type and asked Vasilios for a litre of house red. As he did so, he gave Vasilios a meaningful look which resulted in several generous plates of *mezethes* appearing with the wine, the kind of light food that is customary in Greece when people drink, but Vasilios had rightly been lavish with the quantity.

"How old are you now, Martin?" asked Ben, swallowing a generous mouthful of wine.

"Thirty-nine. Actually, forty would be more accurate."

At least that made Ben laugh. "I do remember the difference in our ages, so you wouldn't have got away it. There's four years between us. Who would have thought back then that we'd be here two decades later, on Naxos, with you having found out who killed my husband? Isn't life more than absurd?"

Ben spoke for a long time about his years with Ricky, and Day willingly heard him out. Once darkness was in charge of both the sea and the headland, and a fresh litre of wine was on the table between them, Ben began to talk of their youth. Day could feel the inexorable tug of the past, of his childhood, and wanted to fight it off. He sensed Ben would want to talk about it, and remembered Helen telling him to make what he could of the opportunity to clear the air with Ben, confront the loss of his mother and his refusal to accept Ben's mother as her successor. He would need a lot more wine for that.

As it happened, there was no shortage of wine at Taverna Ta Votsala, and Ben was directing the conversation.

Day crashed that night at the Elias House. There was no way he could have driven anywhere after their session at the taverna. Thankfully there were plenty of rooms in the Elias House and he now owned them all. Vasilios's wife had stripped the beds after the last Festival guests had left, and the night was warm enough to sleep in his clothes with a cover from the wardrobe over him. He woke at dawn feeling awful.

He and Ben had said their goodbyes the night before, promising to meet in England when they could. Ben was due to return to Brighton within the week. Day decided to creep out. He started the Fiat and drove as quietly as he could away from the Elias House. He wondered whether he was still legally drunk. Home in Filoti, finding Helen had not yet emerged from her room, he took a shower then lay on his bed to decide what to do next. He dozed off. It was mid-morning when he woke.

Day was not only hung over, he was reeling from the emotions of the night before and everything that had happened. When Helen got up she suggested they do ordinary, day-to-day things and told him to take it easy. They went to the supermarket and bought food. Day even put some washing in the machine and hung it on the balcony to dry. He kept meaning to open his emails but never got round to it. His phone went on the charger unopened. He considered phoning Andreas but time passed until it was too late. He ate something Helen cooked, and afterwards couldn't remember what it was.

By ten o'clock at night he was so tired that he considered going to his room for an early night. At that point Helen ventured to bring up a completely different subject.

"You know, Martin, you should probably talk to Athina. It's only fair."

"What do you mean?"

Even as he said it, he knew precisely what she meant.

"You know what I mean," she said gently. "Why don't you call her now?"

It was not really a question and he knew she was probably right. Late though it was, he should call Athina, although not to tell her anything about the arrests. He couldn't face that again, and she could be spared it. He knew, though, that she would be expecting to hear from him. He recognised an emotional cowardice that had long been part of his nature. He did not intend to go to dinner at Athina's apartment, and he had been wrong not to be honest about it. He liked her very much, and she was certainly very attractive, but he must tell her that they were not about to have a relationship.

He went to his room to make the call. As a result of his determination to be honest he may have come across as slightly abrupt.

"Athina? This is Martin. Would you be able to meet me tomorrow at The Black Acorn for coffee?"

"Hello. Yes. Yes, I can do that. I'll see you there at eleven."

She hung up without another word. With a confused mixture of shame and relief he closed his mobile, returned to the living room and told Helen what he had arranged. Helen just gave a nod and a weak smile.

They remained sitting quietly for a while, allowing the peacefulness of the old house to exert its usual calming influence. He wanted to tell her what had been said during his long evening with Ben at the taverna. It seemed to him that since Ricky and Ben had come to Naxos there had been an outbreak of madness, people had been pitched into despair, or had sunk into wickedness, or been appallingly put to death. Yet last night, talking with Ben about the distant past of their teenage years, Day had been given a kind of gift. Extraordinarily, he found himself in a better place now, in a way that he had not been able to foresee.

His guilt at this happy outcome for himself was onerous. Only Helen, he thought, might understand. Sadly, he was not quite ready to tell her.

28

Only as he arrived at Halki to meet Athina did Day consider that he might not be welcome at The Black Acorn. It was also possible that the bar might be closed, its former customers wanting nothing more to do with the place. Kostas's brother and sister were under arrest, Sotiris charged with armed robbery and attempted murder, and his sister with pre-meditated murder. Who would blame Kostas for taking some space? How difficult would it now be for Kostas and Anna to hold up their heads in the community? The Black Acorn would be the object of local gossip for quite a while.

Day could not know, either, whether his own involvement in the arrests was common knowledge. How might a man react to someone who was responsible for his siblings's public downfall? Welcome or not, however, Day had deliberately chosen The Black Acorn for his rendezvous with Athina.

He parked the Fiat on the road rather than in the distant car park, following Athina's example the last time they were in Halki. Just as he switched off the engine, Athina's bright red Suzuki drew up behind him. She got out, looking glamorous in a black trouser suit, her long, artfully highlighted hair falling about her face as she bent to lift her bag from the back seat.

"Martin *mou*! You look so tired!" She kissed him and drew her arm through his as they began to walk into Halki. "I read yesterday's *Naxian*. Both of Kostas's siblings have been arrested! I feel so sorry for him and Anna. Is it really true that his sister killed Ricky Somerset?"

Day struggled not to feel overwhelmed at the prospect of speaking about it all again, but knew he had no choice. Athina was already part of the story and knew all the characters involved. He began the shortest possible summary as they walked and only their arrival at the bar saved him.

The Black Acorn was open, but they were the only customers. The TV on the wall was turned up so that the presenter's voice would cover the silence. Kostas saw them and came over from the bar solemnly. Athina walked towards him, arms outstretched.

Day would have given a great deal to be somewhere else. Athina was a different kind of person altogether and embraced the big man with warmth and confidence.

"Kosta *mou*!" she said, and kissed him lightly on both cheeks. The bar owner's eyes were creased with recent sadness. "Kosta, I'm so sorry. Rest assured that everyone thinks highly of you and supports you. Where is Anna?"

Kostas Artsanos shrugged sadly, indicated the door behind the bar as if to say that his wife was beyond, and placed a smile on his face.

"*Efharistoume*," he said, thanking her on behalf of them both, and shook hands with Day without rancour. His speech was slow. "What would you like to drink? On the house."

"Two cappuccinos, please," she said, "Come and sit with us, Kosta."

"Thank you, but not at the moment. Take a seat, I'll bring your coffee."

As Kostas retreated towards the bar, Day placed a hand on Athina's arm without stopping to think and lowered his voice to a murmur. "Take it easy, Athina. He's not in a good place. Perhaps we shouldn't have come here."

"It was your idea, Martin."

"Yes. Perhaps it was a bad one."

Only time would tell, he thought. While he needed to talk to Athina, he had also wanted an opportunity to talk to Kostas. He still felt extremely uncomfortable about both.

Kostas brought over their drinks and his wife Anna came with him to greet Athina, kissing her warmly but wordlessly on both cheeks. She merely nodded to Day. Once the couple had returned to the bar and the television, in which they pretended to be interested, Athina turned to Day.

"So, tell me what really happened at the Di Quercia Tower," she said in a low voice.

He fought the feeling that she might be relishing the horror of it a little. She had known Ricky and Ben, she had employed Adonis, and she had met Evangelia, so her curiosity was natural. Day's challenge was to answer her without betraying Ben by speaking of Ricky's relationship with Adonis, and without compromising the police case. He also had to speak in a low voice to avoid being overheard. The effort drained him and he knew he made a bad job of it. He felt the emotional exhaustion of the past forty-eight hours fill him again.

When his story lurched to an end, Athina gave a small noise, full of sadness and sympathy.

"It's a tragedy. And who would have guessed about Evangelia?" She glanced over at Kostas and her eyes took in the little bar and its sad, empty atmosphere. "Do you know the traditional explanation of black acorns, Martin?"

"Yes, Aristos Iraklidis told me about it."

Athina was not to be distracted.

"In nature, black acorns are produced when the oak tree is unhealthy or dying. The acorns turn black and nothing good comes of them. It's a metaphor around here for damaged children."

"Surely Kostas must have been aware of that. Why on earth name his bar The Black Acorn?"

"I don't know if he knew about it before, but I'm sure he's aware of it now. I can imagine what some people are saying. As I see it, his ancestors once owned the Di Quercia Tower, and then they lost everything. They were damaged and disinherited, and the later generations came to no good, like the black fruits of a dying oak. People will say it's no surprise that the family turned out badly, and now everyone can see that Sotiris and Evangelia are black acorns. It's a legacy from their ancestors."

She stared into her coffee thoughtfully. Day let the silence lengthen. He had no intention of telling her the whole story about the troubled father, Manolis Artsanos, but to Day it was that legacy, rather than the loss of the Di Quercia Tower, that was the real cause of the viciousness of two of his children.

Over at the bar Kostas was staring fixedly at the television news, ignoring his wife who was whispering at him insistently. Day could put off his most difficult task no longer.

"Athina, …" he began in the kindest voice he could find, turning back to her. The look on her face stopped him.

"You don't have to say anything, *agapi mou*," she said, placing her hand mischievously on his knee.

"Say what?"

Her eyes were merry again, like when they had first met.

"I know what you want to tell me. There is no need for words. I can see that your heart's already given to another woman. It isn't that difficult to work out, don't look surprised! I can see what's right in front of me." She was actually laughing, and Day wondered whether her words had been pre-prepared. "I hope and expect we shall remain friends?"

"Of course," he said quietly, further excuses petering out. Through his relief, and his renewed admiration for her, he found time to wonder when Athina had seen him with Deppi. It must have been at the Festival. Surely he hadn't been so obvious?

"And you should do something about it," she continued. "You would be so good together. And with that advice I shall leave you. I have some clients to meet at the ferry in an hour. Let's see each other again in a little while and have a drink, and laugh about ourselves."

Tossing her hair from her face, she kissed his lips lightly and waved as she left the bar.

Day sat watching her go until she had turned a corner of the lane. His mind felt woolly and muddled, and his confusion sat like a headache.

This was not his forte. He signalled to Kostas for another coffee and opened his phone mechanically, less interested in messages than distraction.

When he looked up he found Kostas standing by the table with a coffee in each hand. He put one cup in front of Day and kept the other for himself.

"Would you allow me to join you for a few moments, *Kyrie* Day?"

Day gestured to the opposite chair and Kostas sat down, folding his fingers round his coffee cup as if warming them. Although about Day's age, the Greek had lines on his face more usual in an older man.

"My wife has persuaded me that I should speak to you, if you permit me. It would be doing me a great service …"

"Of course, go ahead," said Day. This was not at all how he had anticipated beginning his conversation with Kostas Artsanos.

"I have something to explain about my sister, Evangelia. I'm fully aware of recent events, and I know about your involvement in her confession. I also know how you were threatened by my brother. The son of the woman who runs the *mikri agora* is in the local police… I apologise on behalf of my family. I think the best thing I can do is to tell you the truth as I know it. Unfortunately I too must take some blame for what has happened."

Day looked across at Kostas, frowning. He wondered whether he was about to hear the confession of a third black acorn.

"In what way?"

"Everything has been hard for my sister. Our elder brother has made her whole life fearful to her, and he in turn suffered at the hands of our father. Evangelia's husband, who appeared to her when she was a teenager as a way to escape our family, was not what he appeared, and she regretted her mistake. I'm not making an excuse, I'm explaining how it was."

"Why are you telling me this, Kosta? May I call you Kosta?"

"I'm telling you because you should know the truth about your friend Ricky Somerset."

"The truth?"

"It was selfish of me, but I've kept this secret for a very long time and now I must share it. First, will you tell me what my sister told you about our father's death?"

"She said she saw your father and Ricky quarrelling in the boat; she used the word fighting. She said Ricky hit your father then saved himself by jumping off the boat as it exploded, leaving your father to die."

"Yes, that's what she thought she saw. She truly believed it. Everything that has followed is the result of Evangelia misinterpreting what she could only see from a distance. She was fifteen at the time and I was nineteen. She happened to be at the far end of the bay walking on the beach and saw our father die. I was on a small headland much closer to the boat than she was. I saw what really happened."

Day waited. The man in front of him was struggling and Day prepared himself again for a confession of some kind.

"Our father was a very unpleasant man, Martin. He played the part of a tough fisherman, a loyal family man, a strong husband and father, a role model for his sons. Behind closed doors he bullied Sotiris physically, 'to make him a man' he said. But I was younger and smaller, and he singled me out for a very different role, one which nobody else knew about." Kostas paused, embarrassed. "Do I need to tell you exactly what I mean?"

Day opened and shut his mouth without a word, and shook his head.

"Even though I was an adult by the time of my father's death, strong enough to fight my father and experienced enough to avoid him, I still usually made sure I knew where he was and what he was doing. I was watching him that day, and what I saw didn't surprise me: my father had taken a younger man out in the fishing boat. It was Ricky, although I didn't know his name till later. I should tell you that my father was deeply ashamed of himself, but he was powerless to resist his needs. He sought out gay men and took them out on the boat where they would be alone. Once they'd finished, my father would turn violent. I mean, he would use his fists; he wanted to punish himself but he punished them. Later, if he could get hold of me, it would be my turn."

Kostas took a swallow of his coffee to cover his momentary inability to continue. Day looked across to the bar where his wife was watching them, her face full of concern.

"So now I'll tell you what I saw on the day he died. Normally my father would take the boat further out, away from prying eyes, but this time he didn't get the chance. It all happened so fast. My father and Ricky were standing very close. After a while my father pulled away from Ricky and started to hit him, again and again. I could hear the shouting even at that distance. What Evangelia didn't understand was that my father was the aggressor not Ricky, he was beating him really badly. I'd seen it happen before, but never as furiously. I guess Ricky refused him.

"This time my father went too far. Ricky was knocked unconscious and fell onto the pile of nets in the boat. He didn't move. My father looked at him, then picked him up under the arms and threw him overboard. It was quite deliberate. Ricky was unconscious. My father meant for Ricky to drown.

"I was frantic. I was too far away to get help. I knew Ricky didn't have much time. Then he began to move in the water and I realised he'd recovered consciousness. He began to swim slowly towards the beach. I watched him, willing him to make it. I wasn't watching the boat. I didn't see what happened, but Ricky had nearly reached the beach when there was a flash, then an explosion. You know the rest."

"Ricky turned round and swam back towards your father?"

"That's right. I saw him dive many times till he got hold of the body and brought it to shore. I should have gone to help him, but I didn't."

Kostas shook his head and looked into Day's face, his eyes moist.

"I understand."

"Do you?" said Kostas. "My cowardice, my hatred of my father, my failure to tell Evangelia the truth, these are all things that caused Ricky's death."

29

It was the middle of the day by the time Day left The Black Acorn. His only desire was to go straight home to Filoti and get some rest. He had slept badly the night before and still felt drained from the drunken night with Ben. He must be getting old. Come to think of it, he felt rather ill. He drove slowly and carefully the few kilometres from Halki to Filoti, and opened the door to his cool house with relief.

He heard Helen call him from the balcony, where she was reading.

"How did it go?" she asked sympathetically. Why had he not expected her to be sympathetic? He was grateful, but was in no mood to talk.

"Everything's fine. I'm going for a nap. I'll see you in a while."

As he closed his bedroom door he shook his head. Everything fine? Why on earth had that come out of his mouth? He opened the window for fresh air and lay on his bed. He was just drifting into a blank and empty space in his head when he heard the arrival of a text message.

It was from Andreas. He was suggesting that Day meet him at the station at six o'clock to examine the stolen antiquities before they went for a drink together at Diogenes. Andreas had remembered that Diogenes was Day's favourite bar in Chora. Day sighed.

He replied that he'd be there, then fell back on the pillow and disappeared into a feverish place of no dreams.

Sleep is the great healer, he thought as he opened his eyes.

He took a shower, dressed in clean clothes, and went to apologise to Helen. When he'd finished she said nothing but gave him a hug. This unusual gesture impressed him more than any words. He wondered exactly how bad he looked.

"Andreas sent me a message," he said. "I asked if I could see the antiquities that we found in Sifones, the things that Sotiris stole. Andreas has offered to let me see them at six o'clock. I'm sure you'd be welcome if you wanted to come too."

"No thanks, I'll leave that to you. You should go for a drink afterwards with Andreas."

"Mmm. I'd thought I might. Would you mind?"

She laughed. "Of course not."

And so it was settled, and Day began to feel better. The thought of holding the antiquities in his hands took on the familiar magic. It was nearly time to be going, and he ate what he could find in the fridge before leaving.

This time he sat behind the wheel of the Fiat without a sense of dread. The roads in Chora were less busy than usual, and it struck Day that the holiday season really was at an end. The weather was still pleasant, and there were certainly some visitors in the streets and bars, but the hustle and bustle of high summer was a thing of the past. He reached the station just as a young officer was coming out, and was surprised when the policeman gave a slight bow of the head and held the door open for him.

The man at the desk looked up. He too seemed to recognise Day and reached at once for the phone to announce his arrival, but at that moment Inspector Cristopoulos opened the door to his office and beckoned Day inside. The room was full of people, and Day understood why when he saw what was on the desk. Three large canvas bags. In addition to Cristopoulos, Andreas and himself, three more officers were present, presumably to ensure the safety of the valuables, and they were discreetly armed.

"*Kalispera*, Martin," said Andreas. "Take a seat. Thank you for giving us the benefit of your expertise to identify the items we've recovered from Sifones."

"Not at all. As I said, I'm only too happy to examine them. Shall we start?"

"By all means. If you wouldn't mind giving us a description of each item, this officer will take notes."

Day nodded, sat at the desk and reached for the nearest bag. He had a knot of excitement in his stomach. Peering inside he very carefully inserted his hand.

His fingers encountered an unwrapped item which felt rough. Not a great start. It was clearly the sharp end of a metal weapon. He brought it out cautiously and turned it over in his hand. About six or seven inches long, its sides were notched with use and age, the surface black and green and dull yellow.

"This is a Mycenaean spearhead made of bronze. Spears were cheaper to make than swords and had a better reach, so more were produced. It's not a rare item. You can tell from this end, here, where it was attached to the wooden shaft, that the head was cast using the 'lost wax' method."

He paused to give the young officer time to finish typing notes into the computer, and glanced at Andreas. "I hope it isn't all weaponry," he murmured with a smile. Andreas merely raised his eyebrows noncommittally.

Day returned to the bag and brought out an item wrapped in a cloth which turned out to be a beautiful painted vase decorated with a bull, a large bird and a stylised deer.

"Ah, this is better. This too is Mycenaean. That is, it dates from the Greek Bronze Age. It's a vase decorated in the Pictorial Style, with images of bulls, birds and deer." He offered the specific details for the officer taking down the descriptions.

Carefully extracting two more pieces, he unwrapped them and set them on the desk.

"A plate with a boar design, of a date similar to the vase." He picked up the plate and examined the reverse, before replacing it carefully on the desk and lifting the next object.

"And this is a gorgeous thing: it's a bowl decorated with fish and this running pattern in a linear style."

He lingered over the bowl just for the pleasure of holding it. In other circumstances he would have worn gloves to touch such things, but the thieves had not given the artefacts that much consideration. It was a rare treat for Day to feel the artefacts, holding them lightly but securely in his bare hands.

The policemen had not uttered a word. As each item in succession had been placed on the desk, and with each of Day's descriptions, everyone except the man making notes seemed captivated and frozen.

Day gently laid down the bowl and turned back to the open canvas bag. He could tell what the next vessel would be from its shape and size. He was not a man to tremble, which was just as well.

"From the shape and size, this is going to be another Mycenaean vessel, a *krater*, which was used for mixing water into wine," he said, removing the cloth and cupping his hand against the sensuously rounded bowl of the *krater* before resting it on the table for safety. "It's decorated with griffins and sphinxes against a light background." The paleness of the *krater*, against which the finely-drawn creatures stood out even after these many years, contrasted magically with the bands of darker colour round the rim, base and shoulder of the vessel. "This is the most outstanding thing so far. I can't comment on value, it's an exceptional object."

He and Andreas carefully re-wrapped the selection of artefacts and replaced them in the first bag.

Day turned his attention to the second canvas bag. The first item he brought out was a stirrup jar, one of his favourite ceramic forms. Squat and rounded, it was a vessel with a false spout at the top over which two rounded handles connected like a stirrup. The true spout jutted out to one side. Day held it with a smile on his face and none of the policemen said a word. Curvaceous and golden, it was an appealing object. There was no sign of the design that must once have decorated it, but a patina remained that recalled the old gold of a Greek sunset.

"Bronze Age Stirrup Jar," Day commented formally. "So-called because of the shape made by the handles. Used for containing olive oil. No remaining decoration is visible, no inscriptions. But it's a beautiful little thing."

He set it down lovingly and returned to the bag. Item after item emerged. He picked up each one and held it reverently as Andreas and the others looked on without interrupting. How he would have liked to have visited the old American in the Taygetus, he thought, and seen the entire collection.

The third bag contained only two items. Day reflected that the American had had excellent taste; the objects in Sotiris's share alone were without exception good examples of their kind. Day opened one of the remaining treasures, the larger of the two.

"Ah. This is interesting. It's earlier than the other things, probably Minoan. It's called a *rhyton*, which is a drinking horn. Shaped like a horn, of course. It would be filled with wine and then the drinking hole is at the bottom, here. This one is decorated with stylised plant motifs. A *rhyton* could also be used as a ritual vase for pouring libations at a ceremony. It's lovely. This is another very special item. Our American collector had fine taste and considerable luck. And money, of course! A great deal of it."

He reached into the bag for the last time, savouring the sensation, knowing he was coming to the end of his extraordinary experience.

He could tell at once that the final object was tiny. He opened the cloth with care, as if he was unwrapping a miniature swaddled child, and took out the small black thing inside with his fingertips. He could immediately see that it wasn't fragile.

It was even smaller than the bronze horse. About three inches high and five inches long, it was an angry little bull that appeared to be snorting with rage. It was fittingly black, and quite heavy for its size. He grinned.

"Well, how appropriate. This is another bronze figure like our little horse, probably also a votive offering. This one is in the shape of the Cretan bull, one of the most well-known and common cult symbols of the Minoans. It could have come from Crete originally, or from other parts of Greece, because these little things have been found in many graves and burial sites across the country."

He looked round. "That's everything."

The first to speak was Andreas.

"Thank you very much, Martin. Any idea how much they're all worth? Just to give me an idea?"

"Frankly, no. The best answer is 'priceless'. You know yourself that some people pay enormous amounts for such items on the black market, even though they will never be able to show them to anyone. In historical terms, no monetary value is adequate. Thank you for letting me see them."

"Well, you could have been shot trying to recover them," said Andreas. "Least I could do, really."

The owner of Diogenes bar had begun to remove the outer seating areas of his establishment in recognition of the end of the tourist season. Day and Andreas chose a table near the pavement and the waiter was with them within minutes.

"Hey, Alexandro, *ti kaneis*? What's happened to the place?"

"*Kala, kala. Eseis*? We've taken away the tables nearer the road, and soon this area where you're sitting will be closed too. In winter, all that is open is the bar itself."

Day had never been on Naxos in winter, so he knew nothing of this. It made sense.

"What will you have, Andrea?"

"A beer, please. A large Mythos."

Day ordered the same, and Alexandros, the waiter, who knew Day's preference for gin and tonic, went away looking slightly puzzled.

"When are you going back to Athens?" Day asked.

"In a couple of days, once all the reports are written and the prisoners processed. I'm not rushing back. I might even take a bit of leave."

Their beers were brought to the table with a generous bowl of salty snacks and two glasses of water. A small tin cylinder containing the till receipt was also placed on the table.

"What's happening to Evangelia and Adonis?"

"They're being transferred to Athens tomorrow, Sotiris Artsanos too. The charges against them can't to be dealt with locally. Sotiris Artsanos will be interrogated in the hope he'll incriminate the rest of the Taygetus gang. Ideally we can recover more of the stolen collection."

"Do you know whether the owner of the collection is still alive?"

"I'm afraid not. He died last year. It's for the lawyers to decide, but I've heard he asked for a certain national museum to receive anything from his collection that was recovered."

Andreas took a long swallow of his beer and smiled grimly.

"I believe the courts will bring three verdicts of guilty without too much trouble. Then the newspapers will go mad with it for a few weeks, both here and in the UK."

"Something else to make Ben Lear's life a misery," murmured Day.

"I'm afraid that's inevitable, but the attention of the public is mercifully short-lived. The same applies to the brother, Kostas Artsanos. This will be very hard on him for a while, but it will pass."

"I went to his bar yesterday. It was empty."

Day had been thinking of telling Andreas what Kostas had told him, but made an instant decision not to share it after all. It would not change the case against Evangelia, and was something that Kostas alone needed to process.

They concentrated on the important business of enjoying the beer. After a while, following talk of his leave and Day's plans to work in England during the winter, Andreas enquired after Helen.

"She's well. Do you want me to take her a message from you?"

Andreas laughed. "You can see what's in front of your face as well as the next man, Martin, no need for such British tact. Your friend is an attractive woman and she's had me running after her like a boy. No, I'm going to leave it some time until I speak to Helen again. She's made it clear she's not interested in me. She seems quite determined not to get involved with anyone for the foreseeable future. I've also got a lot of work to do once I get back to Athens. You insist on finding criminals for me to deal with."

"I don't expect to be doing it again, Andrea!"

"Why do I not have any confidence in that?"

Day grinned.

"Now," went on Andreas, "I have something to tell you which you'll find out from the local newspapers in any case. My colleague Tasos Cristopoulos is due to retire. I believe he will do so as soon as a suitable choice has been made for his replacement. The new Chief of Police for Naxos will be an external appointment, as none of our existing officers have reached sufficient seniority. I thought you might like to speak to Cristopoulos before he leaves. Despite his laconic manner, he holds you in high esteem."

"Naxos will be the poorer without Cristopoulos. He knows this island inside out. I'll miss seeing him around Chora. You know, I've never known his first name. How strange to learn it now, just when he's about to leave."

"He prefers not to use it, I understand."

"Well, I wish him luck. I'll certainly go to see him before he leaves. And what about you, Andrea? Any career moves ahead for you?"

"As I've said before, I'll have to be based in Athens for a few more years, but my plan is to move away from serious crime and eventually transfer to the IAAF."

"International Art and Antiquities Fraud squad?"

"Correct."

"Will that mean a move away from Greece?"

"Perhaps. Perhaps not. Ideally not."

He may have said more, but they were interrupted by a woman with a young boy at her side who was attracting their attention from the pavement. Day and Andreas stood up to greet her.

"Deppi! *Ti kaneis?* Andreas, I don't remember if you've met Despina Kiloziglou? Deppi, this is Inspector Andreas Nomikos of the Athens Police."

They shook hands and Day added, "And this is Nestoras, her son."

The ten year-old shook hands with the policeman with great formality. He was clearly impressed, as well he might be. A senior policeman was not the kind of man a boy met every day, especially one so tall, with light hair and blue eyes and an imposing aura of authority. At least on this occasion the eyes had a kind expression.

"Would you like to join us, Deppi? A small glass of wine, perhaps?"

Deppi hesitated and then, to Day's pleasure, she accepted.

"Just for a few minutes, if we're not interrupting," she said. "I won't have any wine, thank you, but some mineral water would be perfect. We've walked rather a long way. It's nearly time for Nestoras to go to bed, but it was so stuffy on the yacht we came out for a some fresh air."

Day explained to Andreas that the Kiloziglou family were soon to move into a house in Plaka, but meanwhile were living on board the yacht they used to take visitors for trips during the summer. As he spoke he saw Nestoras take his mother's hand below the table while not removing his eyes from the policeman, and Deppi change hands so that she could place her left arm round the boy's shoulder. The child visibly relaxed.

Deppi saw Day's look and gave him a smile.

"Most people would be very envious of your yacht," said Andreas, "and for good reason, but I expect you find it rather cramped for all your needs. Good for entertaining though, I imagine?"

"Yes, of course. In fact, Martin and Helen have joined us on several sunset sailings. We don't intend to stop doing those. During the summer the *Zephyro* is a working boat, ready to take visitors and friends alike out onto the sea and around the smaller islands. Soon Nick will be putting the covers on and mooring her securely for the winter, but next spring he'll be taking her out again."

They chatted amiably for as long as it took for Nestoras to drink a small glass of apple juice, then Deppi said they must go. Andreas looked after them thoughtfully.

"You have some interesting friends," he remarked.

"She's the niece of the museum curator, Aristos Iraklidis; or rather, of his wife Rania. Helen and I met Deppi and her husband Nick earlier this year. I really like them both."

"I should have cultivated more friends with yachts and attractive young wives!" chuckled Andreas.

Day decided to change the subject.

"Well, how about we get something to eat? Helen will have eaten by now. Did you have any plans?"

"Only to suggest the same thing to you. Shall we go and find a good taverna?"

He picked the bill out of the cylinder, left a pile of change that caused Alexandros to grin and wave as they left the bar, and followed Day out. They walked towards the town to look at some menus.

30

Several weeks of storms and angry autumnal weather followed Andreas's departure for the mainland, but tonight the yacht *Zephyro* was swaying more gently again at its moorings in Chora port. The high Meltemi wind had blown itself out a couple of days before. During the bad weather Day had sunk into a mild depression, dwelling on the events at the Di Quercia Tower. He had been pleased to receive the invitation from Nick and Deppi that had now brought him and Helen to the yacht.

The evening was still, balanced between warm and cool, the kind of rare November evening in the Cyclades that reminded him of a pleasant autumn evening in England. It had been dark since soon after five o'clock. The lights along the waterfront showed that some tavernas still remained open, but the local people walking their dogs on the pavement far outnumbered any visitors.

Somewhere in the cabin below, young Nestoras was in his bed. Day and Helen sat on deck with Deppi and Nick, protected from the coolness of the evening sea by the bulk of the cabin and the overhanging awning. The lighting on the yacht was at a minimum and augmented by a small string of white lights above their heads. They were sampling Nick's latest new wine, a white Assyrtiko from the Moraitis winery on Paros.

"*Stin yia sas!*" said Nick, raising his glass in a toast. "It's been too long since we saw you two. So much has happened since we had coffee together at Café Kitron! Hey, no worries, Martin! We're not going to talk about it. This evening is all about hospitality Aussie-style!"

"And Greek style!" protested Deppi mildly.

Day saw Deppi glance at him sympathetically. He knew he looked rather worn. He made an effort.

"It's so good to be here. This wine is very drinkable, Nick. From Paros, is it? Did you buy it direct from the vineyard?"

"We did. We were on one of our last commercial sailing trips of the summer, taking a group of tourists round the coast and ending up on Paros in the afternoon. They wanted a few hours to shop in Naoussa, so we moored up, let them go off exploring, and then went to the winery. It was great fun. We had a good time talking to the people there, and then bought a case of this."

"It's very nice," agreed Helen. "A good find! So, how's the Di Quercia Tower coming along, Nick? We haven't felt like going to look, I'm afraid. The sooner you transform that tower, the sooner the ghosts will be laid to rest."

"I can see why you feel that way. It's all going well, thanks. Obviously we started late and we've missed the best window for the weather, but I brought in some good people from other jobs and we're almost back on schedule. You must both come and see it, honestly it's already quite changed."

Day smiled ruefully. "Thanks, Nick, I appreciate the thought, but I'll see it when it's finished."

"Fair enough, mate. Any time."

He poured a little more wine into Day's glass and offered the same to Helen.

"Aren't you having any wine, Deppi?" asked Helen, who had noticed what Day had not.

"I'm afraid wine's off limits for me now for a while."

"Ah! Really? That's great news! Congratulations, to both of you!"

It took Day several seconds to understand. Nick was grinning and Helen, who had clearly guessed a while ago, was looking rather pleased with herself. Day stared at Deppi as he would never have risked doing until this moment. She gave him a heartwarming smile.

"You're pregnant?" He got up at once and gave her a hug and kissed her on both cheeks. He turned to Nick and shook his hand. He was feeling sensations that were completely new to him. Finally he realised what they were: he was completely over the moon. Helen was asking Deppi when the baby was due and all the questions he was not up to asking, giving him a few seconds to enjoy his new emotions.

"Thanks, mate," said Nick. "We're really delighted. The house in Plaka is just about ready, which is great because we've had enough of this boat. Deppi's feeling sick all the time, which is bad enough without living on something that rocks day and night."

"When are you moving in?"

"Next weekend, come what may. Some of my guys are bringing our furniture over from Syros on Friday, and on the weekend we transfer everything from the boat. Not a day too soon. It's going to get colder next week, and the winds will be back again. The forecast says forty kilometre an hour gales this time."

Deppi shuddered but her smile was unshaken. "When do you two leave for London? Isn't it quite soon?"

"Our flights are booked for next week. Pity about the wind! We brought the date forward when we received a wedding invitation. Our friends Alex and Kate are getting married on November 25th."

"Great stuff," said Nick. "In that case, you're allowed to take Helen away from us, Martin. But only for a short time."

"We won't stay away from Naxos a day longer than we have to, don't worry. I'll only need to be in London for a few months. Alex and I will work on the book before his nuptials, then I expect he'll go off on his honeymoon and leave the rest to muggins."

He grinned at Deppi's momentary confusion at the word.

"You sound quite happy about it, Martin," she smiled when she understood.

"It's not a problem, I'll enjoy it. There's a plan to make a short film too, for the Museum to show as part of a special exhibition. A company from Bristol called Secrets of Art are involved. I think that should go smoothly. Once it's done, I just need to find enough work to last me over the summer while I live here with my friends." He glanced across at Helen. "I'm going to be staying at Helen's house in Hampstead. If I'm very lucky, she'll come back to Naxos with me."

"Do you have somebody to look after your house, Martin? Or rather, houses?" asked Deppi.

"Oh, I'll just lock up the Filoti house."

Deppi was scandalised at his ignorance.

"You can't do that in the Cyclades. You need somebody to go in sometimes and air the house. The old properties get very damp in the winter. The soft furniture will be dripping by the time you get back otherwise. I'll find somebody for you. If you give me a set of house keys, I'll take care of everything after you've gone. Don't give me that look, Martin! I may be pregnant, but I'm not a china doll. What about the Elias House?"

"I asked Vasilios Papathoma and his wife, friends who own the nearby taverna, if they'd like the job of overseeing the house all year round. They were very happy to. Business at the taverna is slow over the winter, and this gives Vasilios a bit of extra income. In the summer, they'll get extra custom in the restaurant from the guests who stay at the house. It's a perfect arrangement for us all."

"Great outcome," said Nick. "That reminds me, I spoke to Maria Di Quercia before she went back to Italy. Apparently you told her that she had relatives on Naxos. Of course, two of them are best forgotten, but she visited Kostas and Anna, and they got on really well. Maria asked them if they would be caretakers of the Di Quercia Tower whenever she and her family weren't here. Isn't that great?"

"Perfect!" agreed Day. "Kostas gets extra income and, better still, he's reconnected to the Italian part of his family. I liked Maria when I met her, I like her even more now."

He sat back and took a good swallow of the Assyrtiko. It felt as if he was turning a corner.

"So, Deppi, do you think it's a boy or a girl this time?" he asked. He was rather surprised that such a question came to his lips.

By the time Helen and he left the *Zephyro*, saying goodbye to Nick and Deppi for a few months, Day had even developed an appetite. They walked along the port road towards the Kastro, Helen clasping her scarf round her. The night had developed a chilly edge.

"Right, Madame. Where shall we eat tonight? How about we find somewhere up in the Kastro where it's sheltered from the sea breeze? Somewhere nice."

Day felt in excellent spirits now, quite possibly the best he had felt for weeks. His appetite was good, he had deliberately not drunk too much wine, and he felt like eating somewhere new.

"Everywhere we eat on Naxos is 'nice', Martin. What kind of 'nice' are you thinking of?"

"I meant somewhere a bit special. Let's go towards the top of the Kastro and see what takes our fancy, shall we?"

They turned away from the dark sea and into the pedestrian lanes of the old acropolis where a few of the shops, having closed for the afternoon quiet period, were open for business again and would remain so until late in the evening. The smell of cooking floated among the narrow paths between the buildings, mostly from private homes. Fewer people were about than during the summer, but there was a murmur of voices every time they passed the open door of a restaurant or bar.

"There's definitely an end of season feeling now, isn't there?" Helen remarked. "Maybe it's the right time for us to leave Naxos for a while. I shall be sad to go, though."

"We don't have to be gone too long." Day was never happy to leave Greece.

They turned a corner into another narrow lane almost completely filled with chairs and tables. Under a stone ceiling strung with small light bulbs, two guitarists were sitting on some steps playing traditional music. Rather than the tourists to whom they would normally play, this evening they performed to a more knowledgeable audience, the locals. The bar was completely full, and the only language to be heard round the tables was Greek.

Day and Helen stopped to listen, applauding enthusiastically when the song ended. One of the musicians gave them a small bow of the head and a broad smile, which Helen felt was because they were clearly non-Greeks, but which Day accepted as a recognition of his genuine enjoyment of the performance. A waiter offered them a small table in the far corner, the only free place available, but Day declined with a polite wave and they walked through the bar and onwards in search of the place he was looking for.

He had remembered hearing about a restaurant somewhere at the top of the Kastro called *Estiatorio To Palio Kastro*, The Old Castle Restaurant, which was not to be confused with a splendid establishment of a similar name which he already knew and liked. *To Palio Kastro* was said to be a tiny place set deep in the stone walls of the old buildings, and Day had been warned that it was hard to find. It was owned and run by a couple who offered a menu from Northern Greece. He only hoped he could find it in the labyrinth of lanes.

A very small sign attached to the corner of a building finally showed them the right way. It simply said, '*To Palio Kastro*' accompanied by an arrow.

"That's the place!" Day announced.

Indeed, the restaurant was only a few twists of the lane away in a very old building. Its frontage was modest, with two small, unoccupied tables on the street in front of the window. Inside the low and unassuming doorway Helen counted at most five tables inside. None of these were occupied. Day was unimpressed, but Helen was reading the menu pinned by the door.

"This looks good," she murmured. "Come on!"

She opened the door and went inside, leaving Day to glance at the menu. He understood why she was impressed with it, but the problem was that he really did not fancy sitting in such a tiny and uninteresting dining room. The absence of other diners was also a very bad sign.

While he was hesitating a young girl appeared from a staircase at the back of the room.

"*Kalispera sas*! Would you like a table on the roof terrace?"

Roof terrace! Day brightened.

He followed Helen and the girl up the stairs. The tiny first floor consisted of an empty room furnished with one long wooden table for a private party. They crossed to another twisting staircase and emerged at the top onto a rooftop dining area with what, in daylight, would have been a magnificent view over the slopes of the acropolis and the Aegean. The area was subtly lit, allowing the diners to enjoy the thousands of tiny lights from the streets, houses and boats beyond. In summer it would have been an open space, but now it was cosily enclosed in sliding glass panels. Day felt as if they had emerged from the Kastro at the level of the stars.

"Special enough?" murmured Helen.

They were shown to a plain table of immaculate bleached wood with white padded chairs and a small pot of herbs in the centre. The walls were decorated on a maritime theme: blue and green sea-glass had been used to make wall art suggestive of the waters around the island. Although the decor was simple, the combination of stylishness and vista was magical. A hum of contented voices rose from the three other occupied tables, none of which were too close to theirs.

They were given menus and reassured that somebody would be with them at once.

This place was certainly special, Day thought. Helen sat opposite him looking serene and contented, her only problem whether to look at the menu, the decor or the night beyond the window. Day watched her as she gazed out over the Kastro. She was wearing a dark green dress and gold jewellery. He surprised himself by noticing this, and put it down to the way she reminded him of an oil painting: the green dress, the gold hair, the tanned skin and the gold jewellery. He even noticed the connection between the colours she was wearing and the sea-green glass decoration on the wall beside her. He was considering whether to mention this when a man in his mid thirties came up to them and introduced himself as Kyriakos Charalambous, the owner.

"My wife and I are from Ioannina in Epirus, Northern Greece, and we are proud to offer the native cuisine of our homeland in our restaurant," he explained. "Our wine list contains some of the more unusual wines from across Northern Greece. Here are your menus, and these are our specialities of the day."

As he accepted the menus Day understood two things: that his beloved 'barrel' wine was unlikely to be in his glass that evening, but that both the food and the wine were going to be exciting. Charalambous gave a large smile.

"Would you like me to tell you a little about this evening's specialities?"

"Yes, please," said Helen. She wore a look Day had seen before: a happy curiosity, an interest in something new and different, a zest for discovery.

"*Kontosouvli* - this is one of our local dried meat specialities. It is cold sliced pork that has first been marinated according to a traditional recipe, then cooked on the rotisserie. We serve it with other special cold meats and regional cheeses. Then we have veal cooked with wild mushrooms and served with *trahana*, which as you may know is an ancient Greek food similar to pasta. Our version contains nuts and truffle oil.

"In Epirus, pies are much-loved; they are very delicious, of course, but rather filling, more suitable for a family supper than for our restaurant. Instead we make very small, light pies for you to try, using Metsovian cheese and dried meats. We also offer our own version of organic *gigantes*, beans baked in the oven in a very special sauce, and I promise you it is an excellent dish.

"For dessert, our *baklavas* is made to a local recipe handed down to my wife's family, and at the end of your meal I recommend you to try the *tsipouro*, which is the 'pure' type, distilled in the Zagori region, and also organic."

Day asked for wine recommendations. *Kyrie* Charalambous pointed to his wine list enthusiastically.

"I suggest the Arktouros red wine from the Zoinos winery. It is oak-aged and made with a blend of Cabernet Sauvignon grapes and two local varieties: Vlahiko and Bekari. Notice too this one: it's name is *Paleokerisio* which means 'like the old times', it's an 'orange' wine, well worth trying if you don't know it. Or for a light white wine I recommend this one, made from Sauvignon Blanc and the ancient Debrina grape which was used by the Greeks back in the seventh century."

He gave a polite bow and they were left alone to consider what to order.

"I'm overwhelmed, Martin! How are we going to make a choice?"

Just as he was laughing in agreement, the young girl who had greeted them arrived with their basket of bread.

"This is oak bread, a speciality of the area where the owners come from."

"Oak bread?"

Day knew what he would hear before she answered.

"It's made from acorn flour, *Kyrie*," she said, and moved away towards the kitchen.

"Acorns again! We can't get away from them."

They ordered sparingly for once, as the cuisine promised to be filling, choosing to share a little of the cured meat and cheese followed by one portion of the veal and a light salad. The Arktouros red wine seemed a good choice, and when he brought it to the table Charalambous removed the cork with a flourish of pride.

"This acorn bread's quite good," said Helen when he had gone. "Aren't you going to try some?"

"I'll take your word for it. One can have too many acorns!"

Day took a sip of his wine and smiled ruefully, knowing he was about to begin another lecture in Greek history, and finding it irresistible.

"The oak tree was important in ancient times in Epirus, where these people come from. When we think of Greek oracles today, we think of Delphi primarily, but the shrine at Dodoni in Epirus was the oldest in Greece. It's been in existence for about two thousand years; Alexander the Great's mother is said to have consulted the oracle there. We know the site was sacred to Zeus from around 500 BCE, and it might have been a place of spiritual significance even in Mycenaean times."

"I've never heard of it. What's the connection with the oak tree?"

"It was said that an ancient oak used to grow there, and that it was sacred to Zeus. The sound of the breeze moving the leaves, or the birds flying in and out, provided the answer to whatever question had been asked of the oracle. This went on until the Christian Roman emperor, Theodosius, banned all pagan worship and ordered the tree to be cut down. Legend has it that another oak grew up in its place."

"What a mine of information you are! Thankfully it's a long way from the black acorns of the Artsanos family."

"It's felt in this country that Ancient Greece still influences modern Greece. The Greeks have a saying: We ignore our ancestors at our peril!"

"Modern psychology would have a lot to say on the subject of inherited influences."

"Indeed. But this is Greece! Oh, look at this!"

A tantalising platter of cold meats and cheeses, most of which were new and intriguing, was put before them. The veal with mushrooms and *trahana* arrived shortly afterwards, followed by a house salad with walnuts and crumbled Feta cheese. Day poured a glass of water for Helen and then for himself, and refilled their wine glasses, which as usual were tiny. They ate contentedly until the dishes were practically empty.

"I wonder what Greek cuisine would look like if there was no cheese," mused Day.

"Impossible to even guess," said Helen, sitting back and looking at him appraisingly. "I must say, you look very well, Martin, better than you've seemed for a long time."

"Thanks, I feel much better. All sorts of reasons."

"I'm sorry you weren't able to have the catch-up with Ben you wanted. Do you think you'll arrange to meet up when we get back to London?"

"I hope so, but we did actually manage to talk about some important things from the past, that night we got drunk at Vasilios's. Perhaps it was good for Ben to think about something else for a while, but he seemed determined to go right back to those years when we were teenagers, and wanted to talk about what we were like and our parents' relationship. I wanted to tell you about this at the time, but I needed to process it first. Ben said that he doesn't believe I was responsible for my father and Julia not getting married, even though he clearly remembered what a pain I was. He could quote me word for word! He said it wasn't my fault that their relationship didn't survive, because it was their decision and they made it as adults. Apparently his mother has talked to him about it. Just to make absolutely sure I got the point, he said it was arrogant of me to think I'd had so much influence!"

He laughed ruefully and closed his knife and fork on the plate with an air of finality.

"Arrogant?" she said. "I think it was very natural that you wondered what might have happened if you'd not told your father how you felt. What a pity it took twenty-five years before you could put down the guilt."

He had not intended to say anything more, but her tone encouraged him.

"You know, Helen, when I got over the shock of what Evangelia did to Ricky, I started to think how her father's death affected her. I began to examine how growing up without a mother affected me, apart from the obvious rebellion against a possible step-mother. I thought about my personal relationships. I've repeatedly fallen for unobtainable women, and I think at some level that was part of the attraction. What do you think?"

Helen gave a small shake of the head but encouraged him to continue.

"I'll give you an example. There was a young woman at university whose name was Ophelia. She was a junior member of staff, just a few years older than me, and obviously the teacher-student relationship was a non-starter in those days. I was very much in love, but I had no intention of taking any risks. It lasted for years."

"Did you ever tell her how you felt?"

"Yes. It's a long story."

"Has it happened recently?"

Day realised that Helen had not only understood him but had jumped ahead, and was now leading him to a specific confession. He found, to his surprise, that he was relieved.

"Yes, of course, you're right. When we met Deppi in April it happened again, but this time what attracted me was her relationship with her son. The tenderness between them really affected me, perhaps because it's something I missed out on. I think I understood that at the time. I would never, ever have revealed my feelings to Deppi, you know that; she was married, unavailable and safe, like someone on a pedestal. Anyway, this evening, when we found out that she was pregnant, it was like being let out of a rather wonderful padded cell!"

"Oh Martin," she smiled. "I wonder if she guessed?"

Day smiled too. Helen's response was better than he felt he deserved. As to her question, he shelved it for consideration at a later time.

Kyriakos Charalambous arrived at that moment to clear the table. They decided against the *tsipouro* which he recommended and asked for the bill. Moments later, a complimentary dish of fresh fruit was brought to them, an orange and a nectarine sliced attractively and fragrant with summer, and a small cluster of purple grapes. Helen tried everything with obvious pleasure; Day, who never seriously considered fruit, simply watched her eat.

"I enjoyed my drink with Andreas before he left," he said. "There can't be another policeman in the world who would put up with me as he does."

"You're right, Andreas is quite remarkable. Despite being a policeman he has the ability to think and act creatively, like you. You're very different from each other, but you seem to have reached a mutual respect."

"Yes, I agree. What about you and him …?"

"We've settled on friendship."

Day poured the last of the wine into his own glass, Helen's being still full. The moment had come; they were the last people on the roof terrace and soon they would have to pay the bill and leave.

"There's something else I've discovered about myself," he began. "Recently we've seen close up how evil people can be, the vindictiveness, the violence, the inhumanity. I can't help but stand back from the human race sometimes and be appalled. When Evangelia told me what she had done to Ricky with such pride, such malice, my feeling of horror was overwhelming. Eventually it made me understand that I had to focus on what was really good in my own life."

He took a sip of wine, replaced the glass carefully and sat back in his chair. She was watching him thoughtfully.

"Then I knew what that was. It's you, Helen."

She did not immediately respond. He watched for her reaction, his optimism and certainty draining away from the pit of his stomach. Their conversation about errors came back to him, and he wondered whether he may have just made an enormous one. What on earth had possessed him? Their friendship, their casual happiness that he so enjoyed, were so important to him and now he might have broken something irreparably. He watched as she stretched out her hand towards her wine glass, looked at him, took a sip, and replaced the glass on the table carefully.

"Would you mind telling me what you mean exactly?" she said.

"I'm sorry. I've alarmed you. I felt so elated this evening, I didn't stop to think …"

"I'm not alarmed, and I know how you're feeling tonight. The last weeks have been hard for you, and you've just heard about Deppi, I'm not surprised you're emotional. I just want to be sure I understand you. Go on."

Day heard the coolness of her words, but that coolness acted like a balm to his initial panic. It seemed he had not ruined everything, yet.

"I don't want to spoil what we already have. We both enjoy our freedom and I appreciate you've always said you don't want another relationship after Zissis. If you want us to stay as we are, that's fine with me. But I think we could have a richer relationship, if we wanted, and I'm justing telling you that it's something I would like."

"Richer… you do have a way with words. What kind of richness do you have in mind?"

He answered carefully.

"I'd prefer not to put you on a ferry or a plane and wave goodbye. I'd like to be a couple, in public and in private. I'd like to give you my full attention, and share your daily life even more than we already do." He paused, deliberately. "Anything else, that's your choice."

With relief, he saw her begin to smile.

"You and I have lived on our own for twenty years, Martin. You do quite like your independent life, you know. And I hope you don't think I'm another of your unobtainable women? You might get a nasty surprise."

Day looked across at her. He gave a little shrug, smiling too.

"There would be conditions," she continued. "Don't expect me to condone your mad exploits, defying the police and abandoning common sense, and putting yourself in danger!"

"I like it that you care about me enough to be so cross with me!"

Day covered her hand on the table with his own. It seemed odd that he had never done so before. She twisted her hand and held his in return. For a few moments neither of them spoke.

"We can take our time while we're in London," she said, "and when we come back to Naxos in the spring, we'll have decided what works best for us. OK?"

"Thank you, that's very fair. Let's order two glasses of the house's best sparkling wine to celebrate my probation. And to toast our *new* friendship. And just to celebrate together."

He waved to the observant Charalambous and asked for the sparkling wine, much to the owner's delight. Seeing how things were with his last remaining customers, he took the opportunity, when he brought their drinks, to insist that they were on the house.

They raised their glasses in a toast, wordlessly. The wine was light and tasty, resonant of the cooler climate of Epirus but warmed by its famously gentle and consistent sun. It seemed the perfect combination for the moment.

"May this be the first of many years together in Greece, Helen, as friends and as soulmates. You know, I think we'd make a very good team if any mysteries should need solving in future."

"Martin Day, you're impossible!"

Printed in Great Britain
by Amazon

82901438R00149